9/13

FROM THE LANAI
AND OTHER HAWAII STORIES

^{BY} JESSICA KAWASUNA SAIKI

WITH ILLUSTRATIONS BY THE AUTHOR

Minnesota Voices Project Number 48

NEW RIVERS PRESS 1991

The publication of *From the Lanai* has been made possible by grant support from the Dayton Hudson Foundation, the Arts Development Fund of the United Arts Council, the Beverly J. and John A. Rollwagen Fund of the Minneapolis Foundation, Cray Research Foundation, the Elizabeth A. Hale Fund of the Minneapolis Foundation, the First Bank System Foundation, Liberty State Bank, the Star Tribune/Cowles Media Company, the Tennant Company Foundation, the Valspar Corporation, and the National Endowment for the Arts (with funds appropriated by the Congress of the United States). New Rivers Press also wishes to acknowledge the Minnesota Non-Profits Assistance Fund for its invaluable support.

New Rivers Press books are distributed by

<table>
<tr><td>The Talman Company</td><td>Bookslinger</td></tr>
<tr><td>150-5th Avenue</td><td>2402 University Avenue</td></tr>
<tr><td>New York, NY 10011</td><td>St. Paul, MN 55114</td></tr>
</table>

From the Lanai and other Hawaii Stories has been manufactured in the United States of America for New Rivers Press (C. W. Truesdale, Editor/Publisher), 420 N. 5th Street/Suite 910, Minneapolis, MN 55401 in a first edition of 1,200 copies.

For Keiko, Kenji, Yeiko and Neal — sansei,
the third generation

CONTENTS

ORIBU

Hawaii, 1946

THREE MONTHS I cooked for the Finches — Myra and Oliver Finch.

Carmen Machado at the employment office recommended me for the job, then the Mrs. herself interviewed me.

First off, she asked me if I wanted to wear a uniform on the job. Said she had uniforms from maids before but I said No, I'll bring my own white apron from home. Okay, she said, Just be sure it's clean. Just like that she told me.

Can you cook? she asked me. Sure, I said, I worked for the Blue Surf Hotel for two years. Before that, I did short orders for Kau Kau Korner.

Okay, she said, You come at seven every morning Mondays through Saturdays. Sunday is your day off. You leave after cleaning up the dinner dishes. There are only two of us ordinarily. Sometimes I invite a few friends over for luncheons but that doesn't happen more than once a month. Every now and then my husband invites friends for cocktails. Sometimes it's a large affair but everything is catered so there won't be much for you to worry about. Is all of this clear?

Okay, I said.

Mrs. Machado told you about the pay. Is that all right with you?

It's okay, I said.

All right then, I'll expect you on time Monday morning. Tell the bus driver to let you off at the Finch estate on Palm Reef Drive. He'll know the place. Here's a key to the front gate where you'll let yourself in. Don't lose it now. I'll have the dogs tied up when you come.

That was the first I heard about Popeye and Wimpy, their two German shepherd dogs. It was my job to feed them too.

Does that take care of everything?

Yes, I said.

Well then, your name is Mitsui Yonenaka?

Yes.

I'll call you Mits for short?

Okay.

We'll see you Monday morning then, Mits.

Right off I knew from the way she talked what kind of lady she was. No fooling around — that kind.

When she left, the smell of lavender follow her. Like a trademark. Sometimes I can tell where she's been just by smelling lavender in the air. Everything about Mrs. Finch sticks in your mind. She's not like anybody else.

Take her looks for instance, like an ostrich in the zoo. She had this head of real light blonde hair permanented into frizzy ringlets. Then, there's her nose. As I said before, she looks like an ostrich. The skin on her neck looks like rubber but she covers it most times with lots of jewelry.

She's big front and back but all corseted up — Still, lots stick out here and there. With all that going on top, you'd think her legs would look like fat tree stumps but no, Mrs. Finch has the nicest slim legs like Eleanor Powell. Really looks good till you get to her gunboat feet, come to a point all by themselves. Even her toenails are pointed.

Mr. Finch, he's one big one too but he's got a nice face. I mean from the side, he kinda reminded me of Errol Flynn. Moustache too. I told him that early on and he said I've got the girl friends to prove it too! Ha ha. He was like that, cracking jokes sometimes, sometimes real moody.

I heard Mrs. Finch tell someone over the telephone that Mr. Finch work with securities. I guess that means money stuff. All I know is that he talk talk on telephone every morning after his first cup of black coffee. I straightened up his satin sheets and satin bedspread close to noon after he left the room.

First day on the job, I can't ever forget that. Carmen Machado at the office told me Mrs. Finch was a Blackstone daughter before she married Oliver Finch. Blackstones made a fortune selling boats way back when Honolulu was just a trade seaport. She met Mr. Finch on the mainland when she went to school in Boston. From all this kind facts, I expected a rich folk house straight off.

First day on the job, when I got off the bus, there was this high stone wall, couldn't see the house because of it. I took out the key to the front gate, opened it and walked up the driveway to the main house. Even though they were tied up, I could hear the two dogs barking already. They would have eaten me whole, otherwise. Talk about a big yard — it was like a country park filled with all kind trees, even with a Japanese carp pond and all. Morita-*san* took care of all this, I found out that day. He and his family lived in a small house in back. Mrs. Morita did the heavy cleaning and laundry. They had a daughter, name was Fusaye, stayed at home taking care of her little boy. I'll tell you about him later.

The house looked like a big hotel I swear, verandas all round, way too big for two people. Little by little I got to know every room of that place like I got to know everything about the Finches.

Mrs. Finch told me she had a daughter named Leatrice who lived in Sarasota, Florida, married to a tax lawyer. Had pictures of her and two grandchildren lined up near the bedroom telephone where she talked to her daughter a lot. Said she visited them stateside often but not Mr. Finch. He was not interested in mainland things. Said he liked Hawaii better. Goes in for island food, things like lomi salmon, saimin and raw fish. But Mrs. Finch, she sticks to bread and potatoes.

Mr. Finch had his own fancy bathroom next to his bedroom yet every Wednesday night, he soaked in the Morita's *ofuro* tub. Can you believe it?

Mrs. Morita told me he didn't feel clean until he had his *ofuro* soaking. Said Fusaye gives him massage all time, standing on top of him barefoot after his bath.

What did Mrs. Finch think? I donno. She told folks who called up Wednesday nights that he was busy with club night.

About the dogs, they were like children to the Finches. They ate more meat than most folks I know. Those dogs. Three months it took, finally they stopped barking at me.

Cooking for the Finches was easy. Every morning the Mrs. had the same breakfast: half a papaya, lemon squeezed on top, whole wheat toast with strawberry jam and a cup of lemon tea. If the weather was good, she liked it served out on the *lanai* (veranda) where she looked at ocean and palms. Mr. Morita saw to it that she had a fresh bouquet of flowers on her breakfast tray, left them on the kitchen sink early every morning. An engraved ring held her linen napkin. Real silver, of course. Nothing cheap about the Finches. English dinnerware. Everything was the best money could buy.

If the morning was rainy, cloudy or windy, I took Mrs. Finch her breakfast tray in bed like one queen. I mean it. She had China silk robes. Really pretty. Colder mornings she wear satin gown with white fur trim. As I said before, always the smell of lavender around her. On her wrist she tucked a small, lace-edged handkerchief into a gold watch band. Her skin was something special — so fine, so delicate, like you can see right through it. Veins on her hands looked like they were covered with tissue paper. Those hands — never done a lick of work, I thought to myself. She liked rings, sometimes wore an emerald big as a cat's eye, sometimes a ruby shaped like a flower, or a blue star sapphire, blue like the ocean.

Mr. Finch was no trouble. I left him a pitcher of coffee and a cup on a tray inside his study. Cigar smoke stinked his room. After telephoning, sometimes he would sit in his study, looking out at the sea, nodding his head as if counting waves.

What did Mrs. Finch do with her time? Once a month she had a standing appointment with Leilani Beauty Salon in Waikiki for shampoo, haircut, hair set and manicure. Thursdays she went for a body massage at the Surfside Health Center. Probably she had lettuce salad for lunch, cause she always came home starved on Thursdays. She talked a lot about her Ladies Kokua Klub, helping hands bunch of society-type ladies. They gave things to poor people, baby blankets, food baskets, fold bandages for Red Cross, things like that. Then at least one hour every day she spent talking on the phone to her best friend Marlee Crandon. *Haoles* good for yak yak. They saw each other for coffee or tea every week. Still, they had more to talk about. Beats me.

Shopping took a lot of her time too. She drove her Cadillac all over the place buying stuff.

Dinners were served in the breakfast nook as she called the room next to the kitchen. The bigger dining room was for large dinner parties. Their table always looked like banquet with fresh flowers, shiny silverware, sparkling dishes, electric candle lights, glass chandelier above — just like in the movies.

At six o'clock Mrs. Finch rang the brass dinner bell as a signal for me to wheel in the dumb waiter cart. All hot dishes were kept on warming trays.

How are you this evening, Mr. Finch always asked me.

Fine, sir, I would answer.

Mrs. Finch would start right in eating, patting her lips on a linen napkin between bites.

Mr. Finch, he liked wines, took care of his bottles the way Mrs. Finch took special care of her jewelry.

They didn't do much talking at mealtime. I guess after you've been married as long as they have, you've talked everything out. Sometimes he might ask her if Morita-*san* had sprayed a certain tree or whether the ocean tide wasn't higher this month than last month. One thing they talked about more than once was white trash — how you see white trash all over the place since the war brought so many GI's to the islands. They talked about white trash like it was a terrible thing.

Mondays Mrs. Morita came in to vacuum and dust the whole house. Tuesdays she spent all day doing laundry, ironing every sheet smooth, even ironed Mrs. Finch's underwear!

Morita-*obason* is a very quiet lady, keeps to herself type so we didn't talk very much when we sat down to eat leftovers for lunch in the big kitchen. I knew she was from Japan so was ashamed of her English. Anything she couldn't understand, she asked her daughter Fusaye. I found this out because next day she would come back with a note written by Fusaye. They must be very close. One month after I worked there, she told me that Fusyae's husband went back to Japan for good before the war. Poor thing, I said. Yes, she said, but it can't be helped.

I didn't think any more about Fusaye until one day, about a month later, when something I saw made me think twice about her. Looking out the laundry room window, I saw Fusaye out in the yard sunning her little boy. Funny thing about that boy's name — I heard Mr. Finch call him Kenneth. Mrs. Morita say he's Kai. But all the time I hear Fusaye call him Oribu, Oribu. What kind name is that? I asked myself. Later on I understood. Later on I figured out why he had red hair and white *haole* skin. By and by I understood.

Little by little, I got to know Mr. and Mrs. Finch better. She had a soft spot too even though she scared me at first. One day I told her I wanted half day off to attend my sister's husband's funeral. She slipped extra money into my purse, said she knew Japanese collect money at the service. Nother time she saw a hole in my petticoat. When I was ready to go home, she gave me a sack full of her old China silk petticoats. Still so good. I cut them down to fit me. Money can't buy that quality silk no more.

One thing I can't figure out is why she hid everytime she smoked a cigarette. Went to the garden shed where she thought no one would see her I guess. But I smelled smoke — not like Camels or Lucky Strike kind — something different. Funny kind, eh?

About Mr. Finch, like I said, he joked around but he had his moody days too. When he was mad he zipped up his mouth and wouldn't give the time of day to anyone excepting the dogs. He talked to Wimpy and Popeye as though they were his sweethearts. Never talked to Mrs. Finch that way.

Worst thing about Mr. Finch was he had what we call Wandering Hands. One Thursday when the Mrs. was gone, he got real drunk in his room. When I went in to get his lunch dishes, he asked me to come over to where he sat. I could smell his whiskey breath right away. I knew for sure he was drunk when he said I was real pretty girl. Then he ran his hand from my leg up to my neck. I didn't say anything, just ran out. Thought real hard about telling the Mrs. but I didn't. Didn't know if it would have done any good. She probably knew about him already.

That night when I went home, I put two and two together. I figured out why Fusaye called her little boy "Oribu." Japanese people can't pronounce "l", "v" and "r's" too good....

So I gave the Finches two weeks' notice. I told Carmen Machado I wanted to work with more people around next time. She acted like she knew what the problem was. Next month I do short orders for Seaside Snacks.

Sometimes I still think about the Finches living in that big house behind those high walls. I wonder if the Mister ever caught sight of the Mrs. smoking that stuff. I wonder if she wonders about Oribu's red hair. And I think about the Moritas. They still live there of course. I don't think this is the first time such a thing happened in the islands.

PORTRAITS

Hawaii, 1938

ALONG A DEEPLY rutted dirt road bordered on one side by a sugar cane field, a young *haole* man, white skinned, clean cut, wearing horn-rimmed glasses, uncomfortable in a part wool pin-striped suit the color of laundry bluing, got out of a beat-up Mercury. He hesitated a moment before a sallow, wood frame house much like others lined up in a row behind hibiscus hedges, oleander bushes or chicken wire fences in this small plantation town. He checked the mailbox number and compared it with a list he carried with him in an imitation leather briefcase marked Ace Photo Company in gold letters. Carefully he removed his eyeglasses, slipped them into a small, black eyeglass case, then hid them in his larger Ace briefcase.

The man's name was Kenneth Small, and he had the fidgety air of someone who'd just lost something, rummaging his hands through his pockets or glancing back over his slouched shoulders, checking. His hair, slicked down behind his ears and sherry in color, matched his eyes. A faint bridge of freckles spanning his cheeks and nose completed a look of boyish earnestness, the first impression Kenneth made. Together with his casual drawl and ready smile, he invited strangers to approach him for directions to the nearest phone booth or whereabouts of a good barber. Still, you remembered him for looking like someone who had just been dropped by a girlfriend or had just missed the last bus back to the city. He was a disappointed person who worked hard at not looking disappointed.

They had told him on the mainland, in Omaha at the home office to be exact, that islanders, especially oriental country islanders, worshipped their ancestors. A large market for family portraits hung ripe for the picking and Ace Photo intended to reap this need.

Kenneth Small, miles away from home, was on his second job. The first was selling Fuller brushes. He was, however, despite his efforts to conceal it, still a disappointed person. Secretly Kenneth Small had always dreamed of being an artist. His third grade teacher had told his parents he exhibited talent when he drew that prize winning safety poster of a dough-faced, blue uniformed policeman with a whistle in his mouth, standing as if starched, guiding children like kewpie dolls across the street. From that day on, his mother saved all his precious scribblings in a manila folder under the piano bench. In college he noticed that all the pretty girls majored in art. So he enrolled in every art history course, dawdled in life drawing where he saw his first frontal nudity (a shock), loved rendering plaster casts and memorized every art movement, including the new Fauvists and Blue Riders, overcoming his initial shock over Dada effrontery. But after all, a nude was a nude was a nude.

Hard knocks, disappointment, despair fell upon Kenneth following his graduation from college. He tried but could not sell anyone his artistic nature. It was as bad as having a wooden leg. The world did not believe art to be relevent to real life. Four months of unemployment and his disposition, normally placid, turned glum. For six months he sold Fuller brushes door to door. It was a living but it scraped the barrel.

Then one day he read a newspaper ad calling for "Artistic, ambitious young man seeking a future." Ace Photo Company needed a Rep for Hawaii.

Quick lessons with an air brush, a dab here and there later, soon Kenneth qualified as an Ace Rep. All that left him to do was to enlist customers. Photos would be sent back to the home office for enlargements. Re-touching and special effects were his personal responsibility. Not only did it sound like a snap but here was a promised future.

Armed in a pin-striped suit, too youthful and tight for his father but altered by his mother, Kenneth took a deep breath. He dismissed from his mind the fact that its part wool weave itched in Hawaii. For the last time he slicked back his hair then knocked on the morning's first door not too aggressively, not too timidly, but as a self-confident Ace Rep.

An oriental man, perhaps forty five, tooth missing, shiny tan face with smooth skin stretched over a small, neat skull, pulling his eye slits apart from a pudgy nose, appeared. He seemed amiable enough to Kenneth.

"Good morning," said Kenneth. "I'm here about the photographs, family pictures?"

"No Engleesh..." answered the still smiling man. He twisted a cupped hand as though changing a light bulb.

Kenneth laughed. The man was amused that Kenneth was amused. They both laughed; each saw the other as slightly ridiculous.

"Is there someone at home who speaks English?" asked Kenneth, gesturing like someone pulling taffy from his mouth.

The man hesitated, then yelled to someone clattering dishes in a back room. Kenneth gave his necktie a tug and fingered coins in his pocket, snapping them together restlessly.

A young girl he guessed to be about his age came to the door, wiping her hands on a rice-sack dishtowel. "You selling something?" she asked.

Immediately he was struck by her face of innocence. Was it the trusting eyes, small glittering bits of coal, or was it her mouth parted as though tasting something sweet? "Ah, may I come in for a minute?"

Glancing at her father she opened the door wider for Kenneth to enter. They seated themselves on heavy, upright wood chairs smelling of furniture polish. The lamp lit room was stuffy and dark due to heavy cretonne curtains drawn against the sun.

"I represent the Ace Photo Company," he began. "We take old family photos, even faded or torn ones, and restore them by our own secret process. Then we add a little color — not too much you understand, just enough to give the picture some life. We frame it under glass — You should see the results. It's something you can pass onto your children's children. Worth every penny, I promise."

The girl and her father sat and listened as though the stranger were delivering a sermon. The old man's face disclosed neither interest nor disinterest, but the girl was rapt with attention.

"Would you like to see a sample of our work?"

"Sure," she blurted, tipped on the edge of her chair. She gave her attention to Kenneth as though he were the most interesting speaker on earth about to deliver an oracle of sorts.

"Okay. I have a sample in my car. Won't take but a minute to run out and get it — The Ichikawas made one. Know them? Ichikawas? Live down the road a bit."

The girl shook her head. "Ichikawa," she repeated to her father but he too shook his head.

Kenneth returned with the company masterpiece. Roughly two feet high, its massive oval mold framed a somber-looking man in a defensive pose of honorable patriach. A backround faintly tinted lavender and green suggested either a patterned curtain or amorphous, floating flora. Hoping to surmise his reaction to the portrait, Kenneth looked first to the man but nary a muscle twitched on an inscrutable face. Waving her slim fingers back and forth between her father and the portrait, the girl chattered in Japanese. She nodded several times. It seemed to Kenneth that she had coaxed her father out of his initial hesitation. Finally, when he nodded, she smiled. "Yes, we would be interested," she said. "My father says we have old photgraphs of Grandfather and Grandmother. We also have an uncle, a military man in our family. . . ."

Seated with the pair at the kitchen table, Kenneth filled out an Ace order form in triplicate. The girl followed his labored writing, his loops round like a child's, deliberate and slow, a sharp contrast to her own tiny, slanted letters like a fine chain. When all the particulars were settled, handshakes sealed the matter.

"It'll be about two months," he informed them. "As soon as your picture's ready, I'll bring it." All parties smiled satisfaction.

Kenneth left his business card with the girl, in case they might know of others who would be interested. Accepting the card, the girl said "My name is Namiye, Namiye Hamada." Then she added cryptically, "I have always wanted to be an artist too."

※ ※ ※

Two and a half months later (the shipment was delayed) Kenneth returned to the Hamada household. This time he was greeted at the door by Mrs. Hamada, a tiny, aproned woman frazzled by over-work. She acknowledged him politely with a lip bite, appearing to know of his mission, and opened the screen door. Once inside, he noted the lamp lit as before and the four chairs, staunch in the same forbidding postures. He waited.

Voices emanated from in back as he studied the room's only wall adornment, last year's Kunimoto Dry Goods calendar featuring a kimonoed doll sporting a hat like a red parasol. A crocheted doily broke the ponderous severity of table and chairs placed squarely in the middle of the floor. From the kitchen wafted odors — something of the ocean, seafood perhaps.

He was introduced to Namiye's mother and an older brother named Masashi while old Hamada-*san* remained in the background. As if unveiling a long-awaited statue, he showed them the finished Ace portrait of their grandfather. They were delighted, Kenneth was pleased to discover, especially the older man who nodded his head several times, which was effusive commentary for him. But it was Namiye's approval that most interested Kenneth, for he had kept in mind her parting words about wanting to be an artist too.

She fingered the old frame. "Strong," she said, "This is good wood."

Why was it that only *her* praise among the twenty or so customers he enlisted from this plantation, mattered to him? Was he reading too much or was she a soulmate, a fellow artist he searched?

Namiye, after others in her family had left the room, gave him particulars for their next order, grandmother's portrait.

"I'll try to get it sooner this time," he said. "This month I happened to be swamped with back orders but I'll work on yours before the others." He looked cooler, relaxed in his shirtsleeves Namiye thought, not choked in a suit the way he looked the first time. "My father will like that," she remarked. As she spoke he noted a silver barrette parting her hair like a curtain sash. He snapped shut his Ace briefcase and tucked a pencil in his breast pocket. "Well, in a few weeks then," he said, offering his hand diffidently.

"Say. . . I wonder. . ." said Namiye in the tiny voice of a child who at last is given opportunity to talk. "I wonder if some time I could come to watch you do your art work?"

"Wha. . .what? My art work?" he gulped, stifling a chuckle. "You mean the photo-retouching?"

"Yes," she blurted, then wondered if she had said something amiss. He seemed surprised.

"Sure thing. . .anytime, I mean about coming over to my place," he said, scarcely believing her words. "You have my card."

She nodded. "You gave it to me the first day. You rent the Kikuchi's back apartment on Hanapopo Street, next door to the poi factory."

He grinned, tickled to hear her disclosure. "You seem to know everything."

"Theresa, Kikuchi's girl, says you paint every morning, make calls, then go for a walk after supper."

"You *do* know everything," he grinned. "Does Theresa say I have a girlfriend too?" he teased.

"No, not yet anyhow," Namiye answered, "Though Theresa says you are one good looking *haole* boy."

"What else does Theresa say?"

"That's about all, I guess."

She stood about an arm's length from him. Kenneth liked the plainness about Namiye, her hair straight and black, clipped back behind her ears. She wore a simple cotton frock patterned with faded pastel flowers. Her bare feet, tanned to the toes, were thrust into thongs. She looked delicate and clean and guileless.

✳ ✳ ✳

Next day she visited his apartment. She watched him at his easel, wearing eyeglasses she had not realized he needed, spraying pink and lavender backrounds, tinting rose on women's lips and cheeks. He removed scars, straightened a crooked mustache, whitened discolored teeth, filled in a too sparse eyebrow and blurred a pronounced Adam's apple.

In contrast to his wide-shouldered frame, she noted that his hands, as they guided the airbrush, were small and tapered, more like a woman's. Talk was easy between them here. Unlike men she knew, he was unafraid to voice his feelings: "The girls back home — at least in my hometown — wore too much lipstick, too much jewelry. Just went overboard for the glitzy stuff.

"You take a real classy lady, she gives you only a preview of what she's got back home.

"My sister and I are real close, pals you might say. We used to practice dancing together at home. She gave me my first lesson in how to ask a girl for a date.

"I wouldn't say my father and I are close but we have respect for each other. He's good at bowling — but he never understood my art. Only my mom did."

Had he been one of her brother Masashi's friends, he would be considered a sissy, of that she was certain.

Kenneth, on the other hand, valued hers as the only meaningful friendship he had made in all the months at work here. Shortly after she met him she borrowed art books from the library which she diligently studied. She taught him the art of tapa with its mulberry strands stained with pleasing brown patterns. Eagerly he awaited her next visit. All very innocent but what to them seemed proper, Mrs. Kikuchi, his landlady disapproved of. It was she who mentioned to Mrs. Hamada one day at the Sumida Grocers that she saw Namiye too frequently in the *haole*'s apartment. No look good.

* * *

The day he arrived to deliver the Hamada Grandmother's portrait, he felt for the first time since arriving in the islands that he no longer was a *Malihini* or a stranger, but a *Kamaaina* or old-timer. To celebrate, he wore an aloha shirt, the first he dared purchase from Hop Sing's Dry Goods Store in downtown Lunalilo. As he knocked at the door, relaxed and comfortably dressed at last, he felt good about himself, certain that the Hamadas would share his excitement once they saw the new portrait.

His first knock went unanswered. He knocked again. Still no one answered. Strange, he thought, someone must be home. I see a car parked in back beneath the pandana tree. Just as he was about to call out Namiye's name, suddenly the door was jerked open. It was Mr. Hamada, his face red, his voice choking:

> "No moh peecture!"
> "No moh peecture!"
> "No moh peecture!"
> "No moh peecture!" he shouted and shouted.

Kenneth ran to his parked Mercury, accelerated its engine and drove away as fast as he could, cursing life that imitated art.

THE HERMIT

LUNALILO FRINGED a horseshoe harbor where inter-island steamships docked. More important to its townsfolk was the fish market where the rhythm of daily activities clocked itself to the comings and goings of sea farmers. Large commercial vessels manned by a five to ten-man crew as well as one-man sampans left its piers daily with little fanfare. But when a boat returned loaded, an alarm sounded. News of the big catch rose the town from its slumber like a house afire, raising pulses of the half-awake. Knives were honed, bidders began clearing their throats, excited onlookers flocked to the market like stray cats and house flies. Times like these, a man called Ito-*sensei* might be seen partially hidden by massive wood ice chests, obscure yet absorbing the celebration. Living outside the town's confines, he was considered a marginal man, a misfit.

Those not in the know were puzzled by the title *sensei* or teacher accorded him. What they saw was a man wearing an excess of frayed, dark clothing which hung loosely on his spare frame as he shuffled along in worn thongs. A droopy, brown hat completed the portrait of a derelict, yet beneath the brim, given a closer look, was a refined, gentle patrician face despite leathery skin. His eyes were plaintive; he rarely smiled.

My father knew Ito when his deferential title of *sensei* meant something. Early in the century, when both of them arrived in Lunalilo from Japan, Ito had been a school teacher and in that capacity, ranked second to the priest as mentor to the townspeople.

Another linkage between my father and Ito-*sensei* had to do with something called *ken*. Among my father's acquaintances, only those originating from his native prefecture in Japan were considered close friends. *Ken* bound them together. The import of this knot cannot be over-estimated. These alliances held fast no matter what, binding them in comforting bonds of common beginnings. Tied to the allegiance was a colored hoard of hometown memories and a rigid sense of the social hierarchy practiced in Japan.

The first time I saw Ito, I was the only one left at home. To insistent rapping outside the kitchen window, I opened the back door. A darkish figure bending over as though he were a beggar stood there.

"Forgive me for intruding," he said. "Is your father at home?"

"No, I am alone," I answered.

"Forgive me, will you please," he repeated in a timorous voice, "I am here only to present these vegetables for your family." He handed me radishes and a head of cabbage. I noted his delicate, tapered fingers. I also noted, even as a seven year old, refinement in his speech. Where most townfolk snapped abbreviated phrases, Ito strung sentences like blossoms in a lei. Where grown-ups brushed us aside as pesty mosquitoes, he begged for forgiveness. What a shy man, I remember concluding.

When I told my mother about Ito's visit, she remarked "He's always shy. They say he had a beautiful wife once. It is so sad — she died shortly after they came here." At this point her voice trailed, then perked up with "But remember, always be good to Ito. He came from very good family, high class, wealthy too."

That beggar-looking man? What happened? I was full of questions but my mother would answer no more. It was poor manners for a child to be too curious she said, chopping off the discussion — a thing grownups do when you're getting interested.

But Mrs. Yamasa, the town gossip, soon filled in the blanks and told me more about him. It happened this way.

The day was especially hot; the air hung heavy and close. I had been sent to the grocers to buy one pound of sugar. Inside the congested Tokuyama Food Market, an overhead fan whirred like sputtering propellers of early model airplanes. In a dark corner of the cavernous room, among large barrels of pungent, pickled radishes, dried abalone and kegs of soy sauce, I overheard Mrs. Yamasa discussing Ito-*sensei* with a store clerk. It was never easy to determine whether she felt compassion or gloating satisfaction for the subjects of her stories. Regardless, she was a social encyclopedia of the town's vicissitudes and no one escaped her sharp-tongued appraisals, always punctuated with "a pity." In contest with the revolving fan, her voice rose to a shout.

"Did you hear, Ito-*sensei* was picked up for being drunk again last night?" She never gave her listener a chance to retort, continuing, "What a shame he has fallen so low. If his grandmother, the lady of the castle could see him today, she'd jump out of her grave for sure. Their family practically owned the town of Sada!"

I could hear the clerk murmur an agreement. At this point, Mrs. Yamasa, her zeal cranked up to full throttle, spoke excitedly. "Hard to believe what a brilliant man he had been, first in his class, good looks too. He should never have married that girl from Osaka."

"He had that kind of nerve!" the clerk interjected.

"That nervy," she declaimed. While chattering, she shifted a bundle of dried octopus, heaping it atop packages of shrimp so that it formed a balanced pyramid. "She not what his folks choose. . . Such a shame." There was a pause, then the flap-flap sound of her paper fan.

Her broadcasting continued, "Ito-*sensei* came to Hawaii to run away from all that, yet the bride died, neh, shortly after they arrived."

"Sad, no?" the clerk added like a Greek chorister.

"You don't know how sad," Mrs. Yamasa expanded. "He barely had money to pay for her funeral — cremation and all eh? He taught school for a short while then he started drinking *sake* and you know what that means."

"You don't have to tell me," said the clerk.

"Nothing but downhill for Ito-*sensei* since then — a pity," Mrs. Yamasa concluded.

When my father learned of Ito's gift, he in return took fish to the teacher. I overheard him telling my mother about the visit. From time to time there was dangling references to Ito's learning, his love of books, his isolation that drew a circle of mystery about the man for me. Most of all I was curious about where he lived. It was not nearby, that much I knew. Some time later my father offered to take me there.

This auspicious (to my mind) occasion was brought about by illness. Never before had Ito absented himself for so long. It was customary for him to be seen daily as spectator at the ongoing *shoji* games at the fish market where huddled enclaves of players were seated in lotus posture, their attention focused on wood checkered blocks placed atop massive ice chests. Inevitably, they were surrounded by advisors. Among onlookers would be Ito, silent in his vigil but when recognized, apologetic and mannerly, withdrawn yet drawn to the surge of human movement.

At supper that night, my father announced it was time he looked in on the town's recluse. Much to my delight, I was to accompany him.

※ ※ ※

About a mile outside of town, along the railroad tracks, Ito-*sensei* had built himself a crude shack. His garden and hut were hidden by towering weeds and bushes so that one could easily miss seeing the place. No doubt this is why local authorities had never bothered him about its existence.

Approaching the place, my father announced himself with greetings in Japanese.

A frail voice answered from inside the dark interior, bidding us to enter. It took a moment for my eyes to adjust to the dim light of the kerosene lantern which hung from the hut's ceiling. Although he sat up, fully clothed, we could see the man was ill. He spoke of fever in a hoarse voice; my father nodded in sympathy.

I sat on the matted floor cross-legged, slowly taking in details of the room which, illuminated by flickering light, gave me a feeling of being inside a tranquil sanctuary. All the objects were small and scrupulously in order: apple crates held shelves of soft-covered books titled in Japanese, boxes were precisely stacked, even his kitchen needs were impeccably arranged. He slept on *futons* or stuffed quilts. Threadbare with small gold tassels which pinned their stuffings, they were remnants of former elegance, doubtless from Japan. The room smelled of incense and mustiness; his clothes were bundled into faded silken squares. Carpeted throughout with soft, yellow straw matting, the floor undulated as one shifted positions.

There were long, awkward moments when neither man spoke, but this was not unusual. Among the Japanese, social conversation does not flow as a stream. Rather, it is silence punctuated by polite questions requiring polite answers. The gesture of our visit spoke louder than words.

Ito-*sensei* gave me a pat on the head, saying something to my father about my being a quiet child. Both concurred with half smiles that a quiet child is to be desired above all else.

Satisfied that he had fulfilled his obligation, my father offered his final good wishes and we left. Once outside, the shock of the midday sun stunned my eyes with purple flashes. Gradually I could discern my thonged feet and the road before me where the chatter of mynah birds broke the afternoon stillness.

Seasons passed. There were years of good fishing among lean years of want. My father continued to supply fish to Ito-*sensei* whenever he could spare the gift. In return, we received large eggplants or crumpled bags of soft string beans.

It was several years before I heard Ito-*sensei*'s name mentioned again. The local priest, in an unprecedented visit to our home, asked my father where he could reach Ito-*sensei*. Explaining that he had received a letter from Japan containing news of Ito-*sensei*'s mother's death, he thought her son should be informed. Being the wife of a former magistrate, she had been given an elaborate funeral and her obituary spanned many columns in Sado's newspaper.

Details of what ensued were supplied again by Mrs. Yamasa's ever-flowing fountain of knowledge. We learned later that the letter had been delivered to Ito-*sensei* immediately. At the time of its reading, he did not register any emotion but shortly after that undoubtedly crushing news, he moved.

"It must have cut like a knife to the stomach," explained Mrs. Yamasa, "to have caused him to go away like that." Where he had gone, no one in town seemed to know. He had taken with him only the clothes on his back and his books. Everything else, he had left behind, severing the frail thread which ties him to the community.

In the years that followed, I left Lunalilo to continue my education in Honolulu. During a summer break, when I returned, perhaps out of loyalty to my now dead father, perhaps out of morbid curiosity, I visited the place where our friend's shack once stood. Weeds now dominated Ito's patch of careful cultivation. His sweet potato vines engulfed a monkeypod tree, its pink blooms trailed down like a massive flotilla. A few weathered boards poked through lantana bushes where a mongoose family now claimed squatter's rights. Even the railroad tracks had been abandoned. No one could have guessed that someone once lived in that spot.

When I stopped at the fish market to ask a man who was chiseling ice if he had heard about Ito-*sensei*, he stopped to scratch his head. "What did you say the name was?" he asked. No, he had never heard of him.

MITSUKO'S WEDDING

EARLY ON, Mrs. Goto had made up her mind that Mitsuko, her second daughter, manicurist at the Palm Grove Beauty Salon, would have the perfect wedding that she, her mother, never had. Many years passed, still Mrs. Goto could not forget the shabby circumstances underpinning her own marriage, the humiliation for everyone concerned when her husband-to-be admitted that his parents could not afford to pay the *yuino*, betrothal money necessary for wedding expenses. Back in Japan, back in their village, those were hard times, especially so for his farm people and her own parents who managed a small pottery shop. She remembered how they'd borrowed money from the richest man in town, an Osaka businessman who commuted to this province once a year to oversee his investment properties. Without that loan, they would not have had a wedding party, not to speak of the barest necessities for newlyweds.

Promising to pay the debt as soon as they could, the young couple set off for Hawaii. Once on the Hawaiian plantation, thousands of miles away, not a day went by when she did not think of their financial obligation as a harness round their necks. Never again the furtive slipping away at dawn from the village, fleeing the ineluctable gossip.

"For Mitsuko, goin be perfect," declared Mrs. Goto, fingering the hair net enveloping her black, permanented hair like a fine cobweb. Sitting at the family's kitchen table, sipping hot green tea, she addressed her anxious remarks to Etsu, her eldest daughter. Married, expecting a first child any day now, Etsu called on her mother at least once a week to catch up on family matters as if she'd never left home. If anything, the two women were now closer than ever, Etsu as counselor, advising her mother as though she were the older one.

"I want your sister's wedding to be perfect, I want folks to admit that we know how things should be done, that's all," she repeated, tapping an index finger against the teacup's warmth.

Etsu nodded her concurrence. Both mother and daughter had flat, doughy faces with prominent noses slightly flattened at the nostrils and cupid bow lips. Their manner of speaking, wan and passive, as though they sought to persuade by suggestion rather than force flowed out in soft syllables.

"It's settled then — I mean about her marriage to Jin Okubo?" asked Etsu. Jin, the suitor of whom they spoke had been Mitsuko's high school sweetheart. Returning to Lunalilo since graduation from the university, he now worked as animal inspector for the local Board of Health.

"What you mean settled?" A startled look overcame Mrs. Goto's passive face. "American style may be settled, but Japanese style, no. . . . Lots more to do. We just *begin* now."

Etsu chuckled. "What do you mean?" she asked.

"First off, Kido-*obasan*, go-between, must talk talk to Okubos."

"The lady with the hare-lipped boy, lives next door to the Kawakamis?"

"Yeah, that *obasan.*"

"Good talker, huh?"

"Good talker all right. She go-between for lotsa people — Yafuso girl, Noguchi girl, Kihara girl — even Shioji girl with club feet."

"Then how come their second son Hiro didn't marry a local girl?"

"Akiko not local girl?"

Etsu shook her head. "Molokai — the island for lepers."

"For sure? You no lie?"

Erupting in laughter as she taunted, Etsu calmed her mother's worst fears. "Akiko's okay — she only *comes* from Molokai."

"Same *ken*?"

"Same *ken.*"

"Then — everything okay."

"I guess so. They have three children now."

"Kido-*obasan* very happy."

Propping a cushion under her, Etsu re-adjusted herself in the chair. "She talked to Okubos already?"

"Not yet — next week."

"But Jin and Mitsuko been sweethearts for two years or more, ever since she got out of high school. Everybody knows that, even the Okubos."

"Sure, sure. Still, Japanese style, things not right yet. Hard to explain but for Japanese this touchy thing — not nice for girl's folks to talk to boy's folks. Need go-between, more better, proper style. Kido-*obasan*, talk for us."

"Roundabout style, eh?"

"Japanese always go round and round, you know that. . . ."

Etsu giggled, sputtering droplets of tea on the oilcloth which she dabbed with a handkerchief. Waiting for her daughter to regain composure, Mrs. Goto patted her hair-netted head as if to assure herself that it hadn't blown away.

"Why now, mama? How come all this business got started anyway?" asked Etsu.

"How come. I no tell you before?"

Etsu shook her head.

"Tanabe-*san*, friend of papa's, same *ken*, talk over whole thing, say that Mitsuko and Jin going together long time now. People talk. People expect they marry any day now. Jin have good job. Now is good time to work out everything proper. Naturally, papa agree."

"Is that right?" Etsu offered, vaguely understanding.

"No wonder," Mrs. Goto folded her handkerchief into tiny squares as she spoke. "No wonder you not know."

"Tanabe the insurance man, eh?"

"Yeah, that one. He go-between for Okubo family. He come tell us that Okubos want everything — engagement, wedding, cards — everything high class, proper Japanese style."

"So that's it."

"Tanabe, insurance salesman, good talker too, say he come to see papa next Tueday night. He tell us what Okubos say."

"Well, let me know, mama. Let me know what papa decides," said Etsu rising slowly from her chair. "I go home now."

Mrs. Goto accompanied Etsu, waddling with one hand resting on her expectancy, past the hallway to the front door.

✳ ✳ ✳

Tuesday evening, as anticipated, Tanabe-*san* called on the Gotos. He was a thin man, suited in nondescript glumness, distinguished by a cardboard demeanor. From the moment he entered, mouthing Okubo greetings, the room stiffened to attention, with each side erecting face-saving pillars for defense. As he spoke a nervous smile plastered a grimace on his face. Mrs. Goto looked away; she had never seen him so ugly. Would his cheeks crack? He pulled out from his breast pocket a list and began, "Most things already checked, eh," he said. "No mental problems, no criminal record, no leprosy, seizures and so on . . . ." He rushed through the list as though he considered each defect distasteful. "Ah, one more thing. . ." he paused.

What now? Mrs. Goto squirmed in her seat. This was unexpected. She thought they had gone over the list to everyone's satisfaction. So far as she knew, there were no obstacles to this most auspicious union.

"Is there tuberculosis in the family history?" He regarded the paper in his hand as though it were a legal document.

Hand over heart, "You scare us," she sighed. "No, no t.b."

"Everything settled then," he assured her, clicking off the remaining items already familiar to them. As a final gesture, he bowed and handed over to the Gotos a white envelope containing one thousand dollars from the Okubos.

The *yuino* was accepted by Mr. Goto after which he gestured with a slight flick of his hand, instructing the Mrs. to serve them tea. Prepared for this request, she returned promptly with a small, bamboo tray laden with steaming porcelain bowls.

In the closed room, only the sound of two men slurping hot tea could be heard. Mrs. Goto sat quietly by, awaiting her next summons as diligently as a household servant. Her hands, well-scrubbed and spotless, placed one atop the other, lay flat in schooled repose.

According to protocol, Mitsuko set aside half the *yuino* for her wedding gown, the other half to be brought to the marriage itself. All other expenses, it was understood, were to be the responsibility of Jin's parents. It was presumed that the bride would bring all her own personal needs plus household items such as quilts, a dresser and perhaps dishware.

From the Gotos, dictated by protocol, gifts of *sake* and "fish money" enclosed in a small envelope would be presented to the Okubos. To Kido and Tanabe for their exquisite resolution of this most sensitive affair, appropriate recompense ensued.

All of which, finally, left only the wedding itself, by this time an anti-climactic occurrence to Mitsuko and Jin as well as both families, considering the scurrying between parties.

"Have we forgotten anything?" asked Mrs. Goto of Etsu one week prior to the long-awaited ceremony.

"I can't think of anything else."

"Good," Mrs. Goto sighed, wiping her forehead. "Now I can rest. Papa and me do everything for Mitsuko's perfect wedding."

"That's how it's going to be, mama," Etsu said, "Perfect."

* * *

Two months later to the day, the much anticipated marriage, a Shinto ceremony, took place and was followed by a catered reception in the temple's basement. The Sakura Cafe exceeded its usual excellent service (Okubo-*san* was related by marriage) with trays of sushi, bits of choice seafood and delectible condiments too numerous to mention, served to two hundred guests at this glorious occasion.

* * *

A year after Mitsuko and Jin's wedding which all in town agreed had been absolutely too perfect, Yuriko, youngest of the Goto daughters, ran off to be secretly wed in Honolulu to the Miyamoto's black sheep son Tats.

On the Okubo's side, their next-in-line son Masashi, likewise shocked his parents by having a shot-gun marriage to Nalini Kim on the island of Kauai. At neither renegade ceremony were family members present.

MOXA

"Moxa is one of the few Japanese words that have found their into the English language. It is the burning herb employed as a cautery, fragments of it being rolled into a tiny cone and then applied to the body and set fire to.

In the old Chinese and Japanese system of medicine, moxa burning was considered a panacea for almost every human ill. It was prescribed for fainting, fits, nose bleeding, child birth, rheumatism and a hundred other ailments. In addition to this, moxa was used as a punishment for children, many being burnt generally on the back and when more than unusually naughty. This practice is not yet obsolete."

—Japanese Things, *Basil H. Chamberlin*

I GREW UP without a mother. In a way I missed not having a mom, in a way I didn't. I guess it was like being born without an arm — I didn't know the difference. Other kids I played with had that old lady who was always at home reminding them to keep quiet, clean, obedient and respectful to old folks. She seemed awfully important but I didn't really understand why. There were four in our family: my father, a brother and a sister besides myself. Life in general, before I attended school, skimmed along without a hitch. My trouble began as a first grader.

Have you ever walked into a roomful of people and suddenly face somebody whose personality you dislike on sight? It is a distaste that cannot be explained logically, yet you are powerless against it. Well, that's how I felt about Gladys Hirano. She was an on-sight enemy. When I looked at Gladys, all her features combined into a sneer. She had thick lips, sleepy eyes and a pouty mouth.

Sitting directly behind me in class, on occasion Gladys would jab me in the back with a just sharpened pencil. At other times, she would crumple paper in my ear or wave a ruler over my head just to annoy me. I could feel the heat of her drop dead stare penetrating the back of my head. Finally one day at recess time we had a fight over an eraser she let fly in my direction. We exchanged poundings. Her fist dug into my back, I jabbed her shoulders. They felt strangely soft.

"Stop that at once, girls!" Mrs. Hernandez, our teacher intervened. I could tell she was mad by the rooster screech of her voice, that and the way her face turned livid in an instant. As she yanked us apart, I felt furor seeming to steam from her mountainous breasts. Again after school she reprimanded us, slicing the air with a finger, her face contorted by displeasure. "We can't allow fighting in school! We simply can't! You two girls must settle down or else you can't come back to class. Understand?"

"Yes, Mrs. Hernandez," Gladys and I mumbled, shaking in our stiff new leather shoes.

At home I didn't breathe a word of what happened, yet somehow my father learned of the squabble. I knew this because the next day, with a scowl on his face, he told me we were going to meet the town's Shinto priest on Saturday. He carried that scowl for two days.

At the first opportunity, when my father had gone to work, my sister told me that the temple visit would mean only one thing, *Yaitoh*, the moxa treatment.

Yaitoh! The mere mention of that word instills fright in the minds of all Japanese children. It is a threat that has power even today. Comments like "See the Yamashiro boy? He's had two *yaitohs*, he's so bad," or "Last week Sumiko Hashimoto got the you-know-what . . ." were enough to set our hearts pounding. It was only natural that I nearly jumped out of my skin. "What did you say?" I asked, scared stiff.

"*Yaitoh*, of course!"

This threat, this prescription for bad behavior stuck to us like a wart and was largely responsible for "good" Japanese kids, frequently pointed out as exemplary angels by those who thought our goodness somehow dropped out of heaven.

Imagine then my trepidation as each day took me closer to that fateful Saturday. Daily I imagined the worst scenario so that by the time Saturday arrived, I was wracked by a week of emotional dithers.

I felt my legs weaken as I walked with my father to the nearby temple. Secretly I wished to God I could erase that fight with Gladys. After all, she wasn't that bad. I could have survived — but no such turning back was possible now that we climbed the temple stairs and passed the main worship area to a study room in back where we met the priest. He was a slight, pasty-faced man who looked like food wouldn't interest him. (My sister told me the world was divided into those who lived to eat and those who ate to live. He was definitely the latter type.)

Wearing a spotless white robe, he greeted my father, who effused bows and scrapes in the presence of this holy man. The three of us entered a small side room furnished only with stuffed bookshelves. No curtains covered the sole dusty window where a bug was trying desperately to get out. Sitting lotus-fashion on the straw matted floor, we faced each other. I was struck by how clean and pure the priest appeared. His hands especially were the hands of someone who had never done manual labor. They were dainty and small, much like a child's. He spoke in soft whispers.

Now and then I snatched a word of the exchange. My father recounted for the priest my errant behavior in school — first grade, mind you! It worried him that this altercation might presage a "bad egg" future. While my father spoke, the priest answered with nods of his head as if to say Yes, yes I understand perfectly. A prolonged pause followed, so silent that we could at that moment hear each other breathing. Slowly, as if out of a trance, the priest picked up the threads of his conversation, considering the deliberate choice of each word as a fussy flower picker. When he turned to look directly at me, I felt smaller than my six years of life afforded. He then asked about my mother. Father told him that she had died shortly after my birth. The priest nodded emphatically as if to say, "Therein lies the explanation." He patted my head and said I looked to him like a well-behaved, docile child. Certainly I was quiet. I hadn't spoken a word since entering the temple and that was in itself a blessing. He went on to explain that children who grow up without both parents sometimes suffer for this loss by straying from the straight and narrow path; however he did not consider this incident a serious one. Therefore, I would not need the moxa treatment this time.

My father nodded, accepting his decision as law.

The priest, with measured steps, walked us through the church sanctuary to the front of the main entrance. My father offered him words of appreciation and a final low bow befitting his status. We descended a mountain of steep stairs. At the bottom, once my feet were planted on earth and grass, I turned back to see the holy man flanked by his worn wooden shrine, a small but powerful leader of the community. At this moment he carried the weight of a minor god. He had not smiled throughout the meeting, yet I felt that he had a soft spot for children and did not wish to inflict pain on anyone. His eyes, appearing to sweep in the entire landscape including my father and myself, appeared tired.

MANJU LADY

TO CHILDREN of the neighborhood she was known as the "manju lady," as though she had no identity apart from the black bean-stuffed buns she sold. Always, as they approached the small, glass-fronted shop next door to a shoe repair business, hearing their entry announced by a tinkling bell, they saw her. In point of fact, she looked like a dumpling, a compact ball of a woman with moon face and bandy-legs. Her hair, a netted squash of permanented curls looked like a domed helmet. The children reasoned that it was all those starchy, sweet rolls that made her look like the delectible treats she proffered. Wearing an apron sewn from pillow ticking, its blue stripes faded from countless washings, she greeted all with a tired smile. Never one to initiate a conversation, she did, however, answer all questions regarding the goodies with a minimum of words: "Yes they are fresh, No we don't make that kind anymore. New Years? We'll have them for New Years." What her customers did not see was her workcrew of Matsunaga-*san* and his son Yuji toiling assiduously in the back room. Thanks largely to Matsunaga's old country skill (picked up as an apprentice in Kobe) and his fastidious diligence, the shop's reputation for pastry was unequaled in town.

At the entrance to the shop, on a concrete stoop, was placed a fiber mat in hopes that customers would scrape their soiled shoes before entering. Inevitably, however, it was ignored, sometimes even kicked out of place so that the "manju lady" had to crouch to retrieve it, muttering complaints to herself. On rainy days she gave children with mud-caked shoes mean looks for as long as they remained in the shop. As they left, they heard "Next time you wipe slippers!" as they scampered to freedom.

The shop itself, a place that smelled of rice flour and sugar, delighted the eye with pastel colored rolls and small cakes, a regimental army of buns enclosed in heavy glass display cases, their slanted windows inviting all to browse and marvel at the tempting variety. Scrubbed and dusted daily, the room sparkled with cleanliness. It was a warm, inviting place and it prospered.

Hatsu Sugai, the "manju lady," lived in back of the shop in an apartment appearing cramped, stuffed as it was with ponderous, dark wood furniture pieces: a mirrored buffet, mahogany hutch, a scrolled top secretary as well as chiffoniers crammed with moth balls and old linen, all furniture she had inherited from her aunt. A collection of dolls, glass encased, stood like sentinels. Prominently placed in the room was a cedar hope chest Hatsu had been given while a teenager. It too was filled with linen, some store-bought, some created by her own hands. Each item was folded and preserved between layers of tissue paper and camphor blocks, awaiting the Big Day.

Hemmed in by this profusion of furniture, little space was left for Hatsu to thread her way from room to room, carrying on her humdrum life of comforting routine. But her needs were spartan and she was where she wanted to be, close enough so that she could keep watch over the shop, her lifeblood to the community. In a back yard she tended a small vegetable garden. To one side of the back stairs was a wash basin where she laundered her clothes on a metal scrub board. A clothes line bisected the grassy area at an angle. On days of fine weather neighbors saw her seated on her back porch, rocking a chair that squeaked like a cornered mouse as she crocheted yet another antimacassar. The repetition of her days was so boring and unvaried that neighbors could foretell what day it was by observing Hatsu tend to her weekly visits to the bank, tofu store or grocer. If she washed, they could bet it was Sunday. She was dependable as the sun in her habits. Over the years, a few neighbor children who had befriended her, came to her door for treats of chocolate kisses, each dollop like a large tear enclosed in silver. Only on these rare occasions, after she'd plunked the goodies into their palms, would she grin wistfully, as though it was an effort.

Besides crocheting doilies, a pre-occupation which made her neighbors conjecture her purpose — she had a weakness for Japanese magazines. These she purchased weekly from the Uchida stationery store several blocks away. This is why Mrs. Uchida, the owner's wife, more than anyone else in Lunalilo, maintained a friendship and knew Hatsu best. Only the Uchida-*obasan* was privy to certain facts that puzzled others. After one of Hatsu's predictable weekly visits, Linda, granddaughter to the Uchida-*obasan* had asked her "Why had Hatsu never married?"

The old lady first elicted from Linda a promise that she would keep the matter in strictest confidence. Assured of this, she began the following explanation:

"I told you before that Hatsu came with her aunt and uncle from Japan. A brother Masa came to Hawaii later, lived in Maui. When she was a young girl, both mama and papa died. Papa first kill self then she kill herself."

"How?" asked Linda.

"Arsenic."

"Why?"

"Not easy to explain. Sugai-*san* was smart man, had good business head, told how to make plenty money — investments, that kind thing. At first they were rich, then they lost all money left and right. Pretty soon he owe everybody. That how come Sugai start embezzling checks. When he caught, big shame, disgrace. Could not show face to town. When children were in school, they kill themselves."

"How horrible."

"Sad most of all to Hatsu. When she first come Hawaii, plenty people like know her. Match-makers come from all round, I tell you. One boy name was Koji Kihara, came from good family, owned hardware business on Maui. He so interested he come on boat just to look see. Only one peep. Hatsu was working in shop, didn't know nothing. Next thing we hear, Koji went back to Wailuku. Everything going just fine when Kihara folks hear from no-good gossip that Hatsu's folks kill themselves — that was that!" Mrs. Uchida chopped the air, imitating a cleaver landing its fatal blow. "Same thing happen two times! Two times Hatsu not marry because of shame."

"I can't understand this, grandma," remarked a bewildered Linda.

"Folks say it's in the blood, like one disease."

❧ ❧ ❧

Seven years after these disappointments, refusals that sealed a spinster's fate, Hatsu did a surprising thing for a woman of seventy who until then was as predictable as the sun. Out of the blue she announced to

Matsunaga that she was going to Maui to visit her brother.

"Good, good thing," said Matsunaga. "You no see him for long time. Good you go see. You go, I take care everything." He punctuated each statement with nods.

By this time both aunt and uncle had died and townsfolk had assumed, seeing Hatsu in the pastry shop, obliging despite her wan smile, that the girl had at last accepted her lot as irreversible. Now she was too old to consider marriage.

At the time Hatsu sailed to Maui, she had not seen her brother since his arrival in Hawaii. Few letters they exchanged had told her that Masa was happily married to a woman named Penny and that they had three children, James, Daniel and Sally. They welcomed Hatsu to their Wailuku home. While she was there, with a growing family to care for, Masa worked on an addition to his wood frame house, a project requiring numerous trips to the hardware store. It was the Kihara Hardware, Hatsu learned. When Masa first pronounced the name, Hatsu felt pain, long submerged, in her heart. Could this be the same Koji Kihara? She was determined to find out. She asked Masa if she could accompany him into town the following day.

There was nothing out of the ordinary about the store. Open shelves were lined with nuts and bolts. On the floor stood wooden kegs of hardware. Metallic blades and blocks hung from pegs. To Hatsu's thinking they appeared foreign and menacing. While Masa searched for a particular cross saw, Hatsu fingered brads gingerly, curious yet hesitant about the man behind the cash register. Dare she reveal her recondite longing? Feigning nonchalance, she turned a corner to inspect curtain rods. At the same moment she stole a glance. It was all she needed. Yes, he was Koji, of that she was certain. He was heavier but he had that remembered Dick Tracy face of sharp, chiseled angles. Catching her eye, he approached her. "Can I help?" he had asked.

"No, no," she said, her face averted, her voice barely audible. "I'm just looking — came with my brother." She pointed vaguely in Masa's direction. Koji smiled and left. She was certain he had not recognized her. How could he? It ws too long ago. Since then he had gone on to marry, to flower while she had been left with thorny regret. Hatsu returned to Lunalilo the next day.

"Did you have a good time?" asked Matsunaga as they prepared the morning's first batch of dough.

"Wailuku's a nice place — Lunalilo nice too." She answered in a languid voice that dragged, sealing a lid on the matter. Matsunaga accepted his cue with a nod. Taking flour from a canister, she sprinkled some on a butcher-block table and began kneading a ball of dough, pressing down and releasing, like administering artificial respiration to one dying.

✳ ✳ ✳

Many years passed. The "manju lady" lost the spring to her step each time she answered the tinkling bell. Seeming to scrape the floor, her stout legs now shuffled wearily. Matsunaga too, with graying hair and weakened eyes, took longer to fill their quota of pastry each day. Hatsu spent even more time alone. Visitors to her house were a rarity so that when, one day her niece Sally called, people took note as the two attended the annual Doll Show in the park. To Hatsu the event stirred up mixed emotions. She recalled her mother taking her, a rare occasion in her childhood. But they were always glorious days she would have loved to share with a child of her own, passing on her passion for dolls.

Sponsored by the high-hat Ladies Club, these competitions were a culmination of frenzied preparation. Each entrant (mostly girls) displayed his or her favorite doll to be judged. Numbered and arranged in tiers, each doll was of prime importance to its owner. Hundreds were on display, some clad in satin finery, others in home-sewn gingham. There were tin soldiers, babes in bonnets, some in sailor suits, Raggedy Ann and Shirley Temple. Thrown back to her own childhood, the "manju lady" dutifully inspected each doll, pausing to spot its owner, often standing nearby, awaiting the "ooh's" and "aah's" of admirers. Sally too appeared to enjoy the festival as they strolled under a canopy of ropey banyan trees.

After the contest was concluded, they were seen at the drug store enjoying a banana split. Winding their way back, they paused to study window mannequins as Sally was especially interested in bridal gowns. When they passed the Uchida stationery store, Hatsu waved.

"Hatsu must have a visitor," remarked Mrs. Yoshino, a straw thin woman who smiled as she spoke in what sounded like a series of hisses, all the while flipping pages of a glossy magazine.

Mrs. Uchida at the cash register nodded. "Her name Sally, her brother's girl from Maui. She Hatsu's favorite even though she wear little too much lipstick, neh. Too free in her ways."

Mrs. Yoshino's attention had been captured. "Is that so?"

"Goin steady with one Korean boy, I hear," continued the Uchida-*obasan*, assuming a confidential tone of voice. Her remark raised the eyebrows of both customers.

"Cannot help nowadays," said Mrs. Yoshino, pinching her lips together as if to seal a stamp of disapproval. "All kids don't listen to their folks no more."

"Getting bad," agreed Mrs. Uyeno, sanctioning the matter with eyes closed. "My neighbor's son, when he come back from Honolulu, he got all those wild ideas inside his head. Cannot tell kids like that nothing!"

"Getting bad," echoed Mrs. Yoshino, clicking her tongue emphatically as she presented her selection, a dressmakers' magazine to the Uchida-*obasan*. The two women departed meekly as lambs, having voiced their innermost peeves.

✳ ✳ ✳

Hatsu continued the pastry shop until the day she died at age 85 of pneumonia.

From Maui came her niece Sally to clean out her aunt's apartment in order that a new proprietor could take over. Among the antique furniture she found boxes of doilies, the accumulation of Hatsu's pre-occupation for years. Contents of the hope chest still lay in mothballs, untouched as were the many dolls. To her surprise, Sally discovered names inscribed in back of each glass case, fanciful names distinguishing each as an individual. To the end Hatsu had kept her furniture lemon polished and dusted so that everything looked good as new.

One month later, it was learned that, sidestepping all other surviving relatives, Hatsu had left all her savings to Sally, the maverick who eventually married Paul Sur.

SAIKI

FROM THE LANAI

HATTIE CRUMB PINCHED a lemon slice between thumb and finger as though it were a nasty mosquito. Yellow juiced dribbled onto her breakfast papaya, a large half slice sitting like an orange boat on her gilt and rosebud chinaware. After one bite, the sound of voices outside the *lanai* window caused her to look up past the veranda. Crumpling the linen napkin on her lap, she tossed it atop a woven lauhala placemat.

"Did you hear that?" she asked her husband Allen sitting opposite her at the table. He was a white-skinned *haole* with soft, indeterminate features, blonde graying hair and sparse eyebrows. Fading freckles, which stippled and contrasted with his white skin, gave him a completely washed-out appearance. Not tall for a mainlander at 5' 10", he nevertheless looked so when compared to the locals in Hawaii and carried himself with an air of authority.

"What?" he asked, not looking up from his newspaper. It was not today's but yesterday's news from Honolulu, picked up at the post office box on the way home from his job as plantation business manager. Hattie always served his rolled up news along with breakfast just as she did her father in Cleveland who had said he couldn't face the day without a breakfast paper.

"Hear that?" she asked. lifting a corner of the dotted swiss curtain. Outdoors, out the window, between two jacurandas, towered a mango tree. Under its branches, a stoop-shouldered man in dun colored clothing, was raking leaves while a youngster knocked down mangoes with a long bamboo pole. He munched on those he picked up on the ground. The lad's excited chatter, shouting to his father, was what Mrs. Crumb had heard from the lanai.

"It's Hamada-*san*, the yard man. His little boy's picking mangoes again." Her voice took on a metallic edge whenever she was irritated, pinching her brow into a vee of annoyance. Mottled, her cheeks flamed red, the same shade as her tightly curled hair. She stood watching with hands in pockets of her lavender China silk dressing gown. Its folds, embossed with a pattern of leaves and flowers, fell in a stiff cascade to the floor, swishing as she restlessly transferred weight from one foot to the other. "I tried to tell him," she continued, as though reprimanding a child.

"Tell him what?" Mr. Crumb's mind, 90% on the paper, lagged in response.

"The other day — I wanted to tell him not to pick the mangoes!"

"Why ever not?"

Vexed, Hattie heard the needle fall into a familiar victrola record groove. It was a pattern. Allen Crumb, island born, always sided with the locals. He felt comfortable with them. He grew up with them — their dark skins, alien speech and inscrutable ways — while she, mainlander from Cleveland, felt herself a stranger despite his reassurances. "Well, I thought maybe Shiz could make some chutney for us."

He put down his paper in exasperation. "But there is a lot of fruit out there!"

"The point is — I just can't talk to that man! He's so strange — can't speak much English you know."

Soon she will be crying again, Mr. Crumb guessed. "Oh well, you know Hamada-*san*, he's from the old country."

"Still you'd think he could try a little harder."

"Well, I'm afraid you can't expect too much from him on that score. They're set in their ways."

"I know. I'll talk to Shiz about it. Maybe she can talk to him."

"Look, he's a good gardener, isn't he?"

"Yes, he is but. . . ."

"All right then — what else matters?" Allen returned to his Dow Jones with intensity.

Hattie returned to her papaya, scooping spoonfuls of its succulence till a thin, almost transparent shell remained. She dawdled over scrambled eggs and ham. Marmalade was plopped onto her rye toast. Tinkling a spoon inside her coffee cup, she considered various ways to bridge the gap between her and Hamada. With a delicately veined hand, she flipped back locks of Titian hair fallen over her cold-creamed face. She studied her cutexed fingernails. Flamingo Pink, not bad.

After Allen left for work, dressed in a well-pressed, beige serge suit, she toyed idly with her coffee, lolled on a sofa, her legs tucked under a tent of silken gown. Her toenails needed trimming; she would get to it after a relaxing bubble bath.

Shiz slipped into the room to gather dishes in a koa tray. While still a high school student, she had dropped out of school to help her parents finance an older brother's medical school education on the mainland. She handled each dish with infinite care, as though it were a Wedgewood. Three years she had worked for the Crumbs, yet Hattie could not remember when Shiz had ever initiated conversation.

"Shiz," said Mrs. Crumb, beckoning with an index finger.

"Yes." Shiz left her dishes immediately, almost jumping to the summons.

"Shiz, see Hamada-*san* outside?"

"Yes."

"I thought I told him not to pick the mangoes — still, see for yourself, the little boy is at it again." She pointed to leaves and cracked branches scattered about.

"Exactly what did Hamada-*san* say?" Shiz asked.

"Well, he came to me the other day at the back door and said 'Missey Clumby, you no like mangoes?' I thought he meant that I don't like mangoes so I said 'No.' I meant to tell him that I really *liked* the fruit, understand?

" 'You no like?' he repeated. 'Me like, okay?'

"What could I say then? Wasn't he just stating a fact about his love of mangoes?"

Shiz laughed, covering her mouth with a closed fist. "What Hamada-*san* asked was permission to pick the mangoes since you did not especially care for them."

"I don't know — " Hattie said, running her fingers like a giant comb through her curls. "It's always such a problem speaking to him. I had meant for the mangoes to be saved so that you might make some chutney or jam for us."

"The tree has many, many mangoes, Mrs. Crumb. As more ripen, I'll pick them myself for you, okay?"

"You're a good girl, Shiz. I don't know what I'd do without you."

"That's all then?" asked Shiz, nodding her head.

"I think I'll go talk to Hamada-*san* myself later this morning. I want to see how his wife is doing anyway."

Shiz dismissed herself by bowing. The young girl made Hattie feel like a rich British colonist in India or Africa with a bevy of servants catering to every whim.

❋ ❋ ❋

Taking leave by way of the back door, Hattie Crumb crossed a damp yard. To think this is January she said to herself. Flowers bloomed; the yard looked green as a jungle. Thickly flanked by a stand of banana trees and torch gingers, gardenias sent out a heady perfume, steaming the mix of last night's rain and the first break of morning sunlight.

Behind the banana grove was the Hamada's place, originally a shed which the previous owner had used as a garage. To the left of the dingy building grew lantana bushes covered over by rags the size of a woman's scarf, probably a dozen or more of them. Cast over by shadows, they looked blue.

She knocked on the door. Almost two minutes passed before a boy opened it. "*Oka-san*" he called to his mother, who came to the door a few seconds later. Dressed in a brown and gray kimono of striped cotton, she carried an infant. Bound by fabric of the same color as her kimono, it appeared to be a small hump on her back. Her feet were in socks.

"Hamada-*san*?" asked Hattie.

"Ah — Hamada-*san* go stoah," she said, all the while bowing and smiling. The infant on her back began a weak cry. The boy who had answered her knock, had run back to a game on the floor with pieces of scrap wood and a rubber band. A pan of mangoes lay on the floor next to him.

With the door ajar, Hattie caught a glimpse of the interior. She could see that the bed, card table and two chairs had been pushed to one corner of the room against the wall. Over the floor's linoleum had been spread straw matting. The bed's mattress had been laid on the floor. On the room's kerosene stove, a pot of something boiled. She smelled soy sauce and fish.

Hattie, for once, was tongue-tied. She muttered "Nice to see you, Mrs. Hamada," then waved goodbye to the little boy who hid behind his mother, tugging at her kimono sash.

Mrs. Crumb returned to the main house past the laundry room where Shiz was sorting out soiled clothes on an unpainted work table. "Went to see Mrs. Hamada," she said.

Shiz smiled.

"I didn't know she had a new baby."

"Yes," said Shiz, feeling somehow responsible for the plight of all Japanese. "Few weeks ago."

"But I saw her a few weeks ago! She didn't look pregnant to me."

"Japanese women tie their stomachs so — ." She grabbed a towel and girthed herself. "Some time you can't tell they are carrying."

"I see," said Mrs. Crumb. "But what about the doctor? Did she go to a hospital?"

"Most Japanese ladies have babies at home."

"No one to help them?"

"Sometimes their husbands."

"That's all?"

"That's all sometimes."

"I see," said Mrs. Crumb. Now she understood all the rags she had seen on the lantana bushes.

✳ ✳ ✳

Seated on her favorite rattan rocker on the screened porch, she picked up pages of yesterday's Honolulu newspaper. She had meant to read page one to find out what events were going on in the world beyond the plantation. Instead, she fell into a reverie. She dreamt of snow blanketing the countryside after it had fallen silently all night. Silhouettes of leafless trees stood stark as in a photo negative. Pristine, spotless snow. . . . Suddenly Hattie felt cold as a loneliness enveloped her in this plantation home.

TADA'S WIFE

THE OLD NOTION that Opposites Attract applied in the case of Tada and Yuri. He was tall; she was short. He liked people; she was aloof. She read books all the time while he got information by word of mouth, through conversations or what he heard on the radio. He used words sparingly; she expressed herself in grammatically meticulous sentences. She wrote poetry in isolation while he played *shoji* with other men. She was Tokyo-bred; he had always lived in Lunalilo. Plain as your nose, the whole town could see this and they told him so in no uncertain words. Still, whether he believed them or not, Tada Yamamoto ignored all warnings.

When he first saw her, Tada felt an inexplicable attraction. Never before had he seen a woman of Yuri's quality walk Lunalilo's streets. She was like an umber-hued tundra bird transplanted to Hawaii, commonplace enough in its native environs but suddenly, in the islands, exotic. Novelty engenders excitement.

Even the way he met her was sheerest accident. Had he not, at the last minute, agreed to accompany his mother to a reception given by the Reverend and Mrs. Tabata at the Christian church, he would never have laid eyes on the visitor.

It was a hot, summer Sunday afternoon. The same old assortment of locals had gathered in the social hall. Pouring tea was Mrs. Ariyoshi, a dumpling of a woman whose hair smelled of pomade and whose front teeth were missing. Still, she smiled while Mr. Ariyoshi stood close and agreed with everything she said. Straight from the sweet potato field in his back yard, Taniguchi-*san*'s fingernails still had dirt lodged in them and bits of mud soiled his black leather shoes.

Behind the potted plant huddled the single girls, their dresses freshly ironed, eyes darting nervously as young fawns. Across from them two awkward young lads squirmed in starched shirts, looking as though they had been coerced to attend the tea. Mrs. Tabata was doing her best to cheer them up.

Loud-mouthed Mrs. Uyeno, her booming voice proclaiming joy at seeing Mitsui Hirano's new, pudgy baby boy, could be heard above all other conversation while her thin, immobile husband cowered in a gray suit, grinning sheepishly.

Ozaki-*san* had dared to show up in an aloha shirt despite the fact that all the other men wore white shirts for the occasion. Next to an upright piano, young people hunched over a ukelele player.

The Eguchi's were there in toto: the mister with his trousers still smelling of fish market and Mrs. Eguchi clutching a pleated alligator bag, her one gold tooth sparkling as she chattered while her six children bounced about the room in pursuit of a gecko which had jumped down from the ceiling.

Flitting from group to group was the usually staid Reverend Tabata bestowing pidgin phrases of goodwill, slapping men on their backs with pats of his brown paw.

There was relaxed, good natured chatter. There was laughter. In the midst of this sat Yuriko, prim as a schoolmarm, assessing the group critically. She was a thin, pale, rather plain girl with a narrow face framed by marcel waves. Dressed in a suit much too warm for Hawaii, gloves on her hands, a gray felt cloche on her head, she sat ramrod straight on the edge of her chair with teacup in hand. Behind steel-rimmed glasses, her dark eyes pierced as though she were a mind reader.

Mrs. Tabata, ever alert to the needs of guests, was first to note Tada's interest in her niece. Quickly she darted to his side. "Have you met my niece from Tokyo, Tada?" she asked, steering him toward Yuri.

When Yuri saw them approaching, she put aside her cup and clasped a folded handkerchief in her lap. During the introduction, she eyed him guardedly. A head taller than anyone else, Tada was easily the most attractive man there. This was not lost on her despite the fact that he wore what Yuri considered to be an outdated pin-striped suit with a gold clasp fastening his black necktie. Underneath it all, he's probably a boor like the rest of them, she thought to herself as she shook his surprisingly soft and fine-textured hand. Next to him she felt overwhelmed, momentarily limp.

They exchanged trivial, polite talk for a few minutes before Reverend Tabata whisked Tada away to meet a parishioner seeking advice on a real estate purchase. In such matters, the young man was considered an expert. Years ago, he'd had the foresight to invest in cheap, underdeveloped property which had since increased three-fold in value. Soon Tada was deemed to be a man of wealth, owning two houses, one in downtown Lunalilo and the other, along a choice beachfront. He had also built for his parents a large home in a new development area. An attractive man in every way, he was regarded as the town's most eligible bachelor, the "best catch." With money plus looks, folks could see why a newcomer like Yuri would look twice. What they couldn't understand was why *he* looked at her.

Shortly following the church reception, from left and right came free advice. His sister said, "But she's too serious for you, Tada. I hear she reads one book after another and listens for hours on end to classical victrola music." She dismissed Yuri by waving her hand. "Forget her. She's just not your type."

"She's not like us," dropped his mother, a woman who did not waste words, a fact which caused people to heed what little she uttered.

His best friend Yuichi elaborated the problem. "She thinks we're all a bunch of barbarians. Ask Kawamura-*san*. He'll tell you. He heard her saying she couldn't find lace gloves in his dry goods store."

Straightening his back defensively Yuichi continued, "Ever since that girl came to Hawaii, her aunt has heard nothing but complaints from her mouth. 'Can't they speak the language properly? They don't even look Japanese, so dark, coarse and sloppy. . . . And then, no one reads anything but picture magazines here. Practically illiterate. Is there a poet among them?'"

To his friend's warnings, Tada merely shook his head.

"If you take my advice, you'd stay away from a girl like that," Yuichi admonished. "She's nothing but trouble."

Tada listened patiently. He knew they were well-meaning but inside, in a secret corner, he longed to see Yuri if only to confirm his initial attraction.

And so, paying no mind to free advice, he courted her. His attentions were honorable; his first step plunged him headlong.

Dutiful daughter of a Tokyo university professor, Yuri wrote to her shocked and disappointed parents about her serious interest in Tada. "A gem among the natives" was the way she described him. That she considered him a diamond in the rough lay at the heart of her secret plan. Yuri had visions of molding Tada into her idea of a cultivated person. She wrote of this metamorphosis to her parents.

"Your mother and I will wait for you," her father wrote back, "When you have tired of such a wilderness."

At the time his prophetic words sounded highly improbable to Yuri. She was to discover later that her father understood her better than she knew herself.

Three months later, at a small, very private, family-only ceremony, Tada and Yuri were married. It was Reverend Tabata, feeling somehow responsible for their meeting, who officiated.

Once wed, the couple was expected to join the usual Lunalilo social activities. In this, townfolk were disappointed to see only Tada partake in the married men's get-togethers, the usual card games, camaraderie at the local bars, fishing at the wharf. Yuri, however, avoided other women. Rare glimpses of her were caught at the stores where she appeared over-dressed in her conservative finery and long stockings in the heat of the summer. Her formidable, four-eyed stare still froze. Few were the women who dared to chit-chat with her. Oftener, they acknowledged the bride with a hurried bow then sped out of range of her critical gaze.

After the couple had returned from a Honolulu honeymoon, spent largely shopping for household furnishings, Yuri's list of Lunalilo's shortcomings trickled down in small plops. Culture, she claimed, did not exist in this place. Most of all, she missed the live theaters of Tokyo. "Doesn't a theatrical troupe of some sort ever come here from Japan?" she asked.

"Oh, sometimes the town is treated to *karawaza*, a touring circus group," he said.

"A circus group?" she repeated, "Is that all?"

"Yeah, I guess so. I don't know, really. I haven't paid much attention...." He smiled at her and offered outstretched arms, a strategy successful during their idyllic honeymoon. Now she did not budge. "No *noh* performances? No *kabuki* even? No music?"

"Say, listen," he said, chuckling, "This is Hawaii. You not in Japan. This is not Tokyo."

"You don't need to tell me. I *know* this is not Tokyo. This place is not anything. . . ." Swallowing the bitter taste of her own words she ran to her study, slamming the door behind her.

If she had been deprived of any material want in this marriage, her complaints might appear justified. As it was, Tada provided for her generously: a beautiful home, clothes, books, music records, things money could buy. What he could not provide was stimulating conversation, intellectual discussions, cultural activities that she took for granted as a professor's daughter. She missed the company of intelligent women. Here, there was only old Mrs. Iwakami whom Yuri considered "educated." But the *obasan* was 87 years old, four years into senility.

Yuri missed the ambience of artists and musicians who frequented her father's home. She could not converse with women in town; they spoke an altogether different language. As for transforming Tada, her efforts met dismal failure.

She tried once. In a heat of creativity, she composed a poem expressing her love for him, a traditional, two-part verse of restricted syllables. Hung around a waterfall image, it was the product of three days wrestling. She had debated the wisdom of ever showing him the poem. Finally, one day, after preparing his favorite meal, she read it aloud while he sipped green tea.

"It's nice," Tada said. It was what he said of all her endeavors, whether an exceptional meal, a superb flower arrangement or the purchase of a red snapper. "It's nice," he said to all.

※ ※ ※

Nine months later, a baby girl was born to them. Yuri named her Hanako because the infant reminded her of a flower. And indeed, she filled their days like a beautiful adornment. At first, tending to the child's needs filled all of a mother's day but increasingly, as the girl grew, she was left with idle time on her hands once more. Again, old longings for Japan and her parents gave vent like steam from a teakettle.

"Learn to live here. Take it easy, one day at a time," said Tada, who for his part never ceased to believe that she would change her ways and learn to love Lunalilo as he did. He suggested that she search out others in town who might enjoy poetry as she did. Thrilled at the prospect, she perked up for a few days only to be beaten down with disappointment. Three persons attended the church basement gathering: the Reverend and Mrs. Tabata and a blind man from a plantation 20 miles away whose mother brought him to listen. The mother herself did not remain for the meeting but visited friends in the neighborhood. She didn't understand such things, she explained. But her son, yes, he liked poetry.

✳ ✳ ✳

Three years later, Yuri left Lunalilo with her daughter for a visit to her parents' home. At first, Tada assured townspeople with his usual smile that she was vacationing. He had bulky, tissue-paper letters in a fine hand to prove that they were still a family. But six months elapsed and still his wife did not return.

His anxiety grew. No longer could he point to thick letters as evidence of her love as correspondence between the two dwindled to perfunctory notes spaced months apart. Increasingly, Tada frequented the Sakura Bar & Cafe. Frequently he took business trips to Honolulu where it was whispered he kept a bar-hostess mistress. Lunalilo tongues wagged. Whenever possible, he dodged questions about his estranged wife.

"Oh, yes, they're doing fine," he would shrug off, even joking, "Back there, my daughter is getting a fine education. Her grandfather's a professor, you know."

But friends who knew him better noticed a wearied look shadowing his once vigorous appearance. Regrets about his marriage, sleepless nights, haphazard meals, all ravaged him. Explaining things to friends was hurtful; he found it easier shunning people to avoid pain. He fished alone for long hours at an abandoned wharf in Makapa, ten miles away.

Then one sleepy, Lunalilo day, townsfolk were surprised to learn that Tada was closing his business office to take a trip to Japan. "I'll be back with my family. You'll see," he assured fellow tipplers at the Sakura. Mrs. Tabata gave him an amulet to assure his safe return.

And indeed, two months later, he did return — alone.

This happened so long ago, no one mentions her name anymore. No one says "I told you so." They have conveniently forgotten Yuri.

MIKI / MICKEY

Hawaii, 1938

As THE DOCTOR's only child, Miki had been overindulged. She was a pretty girl in a baby doll way with dimples on both cheeks. Her hair was kept curly by regular visits with her mother to the local beauty parlor and she was thin, purportedly because she ate candy and cookies instead of regular good-for-you food. It is true that her father was a physician but even he could not force Miki to do something she did not want to do. As a result she grew up more and more demanding, getting her way in more and more instances.

She wore frilly party dresses to school, the fragile kind requiring equally fancy petticoats and shiny, black patent leather shoes with bows like tap dancers used. She carried small beaded bags or Chinese silk purses stuffed with gum or candy. Girls like myself who envied her hung around to pick up crumbs she tossed our way. There were clues to her pampered personality in the way she flicked her eyelashes when she spoke to you or wiggled her shoulders when she walked. They hinted that here was a girl who grew up nested in her father's adoration.

I knew Miki as a neighbor. Her family on occasions hired me to keep Miki company, baby sitting at night or escorting her to movies. The latter I considered a treat, and to be paid, an additional bonus. As extra recompense she gave me dresses from time to time, dresses she had grown tired of, she had so many of them. She also gave me trinkets all of which I considered jewels. In this way, our friendship lasted through many years and we continued to correspond even after I had left the island. At that age, I remember thinking that Miki was the luckiest girl alive, having chosen her parents auspiciously. But now that I am older and wiser, I am not as certain about Miki's luck.

Early on she decided that she wanted to be a star. To achieve the stardom she craved, her parents allowed her to take dance lessons. Tap, hula and ballet after school became necessities. On Saturday, a special singing teacher drove to her home. What with performances for these various classes, her time was spent largely at rehearsals, shopping for costumes, trying on new make-up, sitting under a hair dryer or taking trips to various auditoriums. All called for the indulgence of her mother who bent her time to accommodate Miki's wishes. No sooner was one performance completed then another waited in the wings. Short of an emergency call, however, both parents dutifully attended all of Miki's programs and were seen in the front row, beaming at their burgeoning starlet.

At sixteen Miki decided that she didn't want to look Japanese any longer so she set about changing her image. Firstly she changed her name from Miki Naito to Mickey Nightoh then she peroxided her black hair to a bright cinnamon brown. She persuaded her father, the good doctor, to send her to Japan for plastic surgery on her eyelids. In the twinkling of one operating session, she had her epicanthic fold altered to a double fold, giving her the deep set eyes of a *haole*. Another surgeon implanted silicone breasts for a full womanly figure and still another straightened out her bowed legs.

It was a completely reconstructed Mickey who returned to Hawaii and we friends who had known her as Miki, were startled at the change. Now we couldn't say for certain what she looked like. There was still a trace of the oriental about her, but then again, she had transformed herself into another person. Mickey also came back laden with suitcases of evening gowns to launch her career as Nightclub Singer. She hoped to blast the world of entertainment like a Chinese firecracker.

I accompanied Mickey to her first auditioning and it was not exactly an explosion. There'd been an ad in our local paper for a vocalist try-out at the Holo Holo Inn. Now the Holo Holo Inn was what you might call semi-seedy; in fact bankruptcy had been whispered about its flagging business. Formerly a warehouse, the wood frame building had been hastily thatched with lauhala giving it a vaguely native look.

The dimly lit red and black interior had a few coconuts dangling from its ceiling. Musicians of a small local orchestra huddled in one corner of the dining and dancing room where a piano flanked a small, raised circular stage. About a dozen girls of all hues had come to the audition. Some of them, we recognized as experienced performers. Mickey sensed that the competition would be stiff, and that winning would not be a pushover. To any observer appraising the lineup that day, she stood out simply by her outlandish strapless evening gown. Next to her the other girls in their informal slacks and cotton blouses paled.

The first to audition was a sleek Chinese charmer who dazzled all with "I Don't Want to Set the World on Fire." A Filipino stunner followed with "Maybe," wrenching every drop of torch singing. Mickey could not ignore the competition; she squirmed. Like a panther, a Korean lass slinked across the stage, giving new meaning to the lyrics "I'll Be Loving You Always." Then a Puerto Rican beauty had the room bouncing with "Up the Lazy River" rendered in a husky, fetching voice.

"Okay, who's next please?" asked the bandleader, a beanpole slim, moustached guy who motioned to Mickey.

"My turn?" she giggled, pointing one hand to herself, the other fluffing up her curls. She turned on that little girl voice which I knew so well. It brought out the latent Tarzan in men, a sudden protectiveness toward a stray kitten. This bandleader was no exception.

Before singing, she wiggled her way over to the piano player, bent over to whisper something in his ear, then slinked back winking. The man's arm flopped over the keyboard, sounding a jumble of notes.

Microphone clutched in her manicured hand, she began to sing "Boop Boop Ditum Datum Watum Choo." She had chosen an appropriately insipid vehicle for her cutesy voice. Her thin presentation did not impress the orchestra members but the leader, waving tempo, kept his eyes glued on her. Sensing this, she sang for him alone, fastening her Betty Boop charm onto him like an anaconda wrapping its hapless victim. Her strapless gown helped.

Confident that she had mesmerized him, Mickey felt fairly certain that the job was all but delivered to her. It came then, as a great disappointment when on the next weekend, the club advertised its new singer to be Consuelo Diaz, the songbird from Kauai. Her ego wounded, Mickey did not heal easily. Rarely having had to wrestle with defeat before, she was paralyzed. How could any of those girls without her class or training edge her out of the competition?

Mickey moped about the house, too hurt to whimper. She didn't comb her hair for three days. The sight of his lugubrious daughter, sulking, endlessly buffing her fingernails, gnawed on the heart of her father who immediately sought to remedy the situation in the best way he knew. Within a matter of weeks, he, through his lawyer and financial advisor, secretly negotiated a monetary shot in the arm for the Holo Holo. Under new management, it announced a complete re-modeling. The next thing we knew, the Cherry Blossom Night Club had bloomed. The thatched roof had been replaced by a fake pagoda entrance and while the red and black decor was kept, coconuts were replaced by Japanese paper lanterns. But most to our astonishment, it opened featuring a new vocalist named Mickey Nightoh.

She continued to climb the ladder of success in this manner, each rung elevating her to top billing. Quickly her ambition outgrew the small towns of our little island; she headed for Honolulu, the pinnacle. This move broke her father's heart, to see his daughter leave home. But he consoled himself by adding new pages to the oversize scapbook he kept on their anxious daughter. I remember its padded cover embellished with a large pink bow and how delightedly he would turn its pages for every visitor to their home.

The next time I read about Mickey, she was front page news in an article entitled "Swinging Couple Returns to Islands from Japan," covering her marriage to Tokyo's pop singing idol Toru Sato. I attended one of his concerts largely out of curiosity to see for myself what kind of husband Mickey had selected. He was, as the papers said, squeaky clean with his toothpaste ad smile, boy scout manners and much humility. I think it was this innocent blandness about him that bored his Honolulu audiences because his voice itself, though lacking verve, was pleasant in a lullabyish way. At any rate, his singing engagements did not arouse the screaming and adulation he had expected. Consequently, his appearances dwindled as his consumption of *sake* increased. Local gossip columns were quick to report a rift between the dreamland Nightoh-Sato duo.

Within a year, Toru returned to Tokyo where reportedly SRO crowds welcomed the crooner back. Then, just as he rose in the Tokyo platter charts, the tragic and puzzling news broke of "self-inflicted wounds" which put an end to his young life. Mickey did not attend his funeral. Instead, she sent her father to represent the family.

Within a speedy three months, she took on husband No. 2. He was Senzo Ozaki, a Tokyo financier who had gone to Honolulu on a look-see venture. His enterprising eyes were instantly blinded by Mickey. Theirs seemed to be a marriage tailor-made for her: he supplied the hotels and she was guaranteed star-billing in their nightly shows. On the surface, that is what appeared to be the case; but not being in contact with her during that marriage, I didn't know what really happened. Newspaper articles were my only source of information. From their pages I learned that the name of Senzo Ozaki was being allied with embezzlement, swindle and other slippery doings. One by one, ownership of his hotels changed hands; his empire crashed and with it, his songbird wife. His story ended grimly with discovery of his body in a hotel room, a pistol shot to his head.

Four months after the grisly disclosure, I was surprised to receive a phone call from Mickey. Between appointments with a manicurist and a masseuse, she wondered if I might be free to lunch with her. Of course, I accepted. Following her life story had become as interesting as a romantic novel, so we agreed to meet in the Lehua room of the Leilani Hotel.

The doll face, the essential Miki was still there beneath the beehive hair-do, rhinestone jewelry and pancake make-up. Light crow's feet webbed the corners of her eyes, yet she could by sheer choice of onstage clothes and manners still attract attention.

Our table conversation skimmed delicately over her turbulent past. Instead, she with her characteristic froth talk, directed it to her future.

"There's a nice Hong Kong banker who is taking me out for a 9-course dinner tonight. Cute. You should see him. Loaded with money too!" She rolled her eyes heavenward and twisted her three jade bracelets.

That cute man was named Toy Wing Ching and he became husband No. 3 for Mickey. According to the papers, she intended to give up her career for him — which she did — for exactly one year, as I learned later.

After her third marriage — Mickey swears she neither knew nor suspected Toy Wing's involvement with the opium business — she appeared to have gone to pieces. Perhaps her Dior wardrobe and Gucci shoes no longer offered fulfillment. Perhaps hundreds of hours spent under a hair dryer, chatting to a manicurist, finally struck her as vacuous. At any rate, in her last postcard from Paris, she wrote of starting a new life with a "darling" French psychiatrist, who promised to cure her of all troubles.

The next source of information about Mickey was the tabloids. Her body, along with a "prominent" doctor's, was found in his Paris apartment. Drugs were presumed to be the cause of death.

In Lunalilo, Dr. Naito, now retired, grows increasingly reclusive. The rare visitor to his home says the pink scrapbook on the coffee table is gone.

THE BARBER'S DAUGHTER

Downtown Mamo street where the Miyako Hotel was located looked shabby. Day or night, glum vagrants loitered alongside bars, tattoo and pawn shops. The hotel's *ROOMS FOR RENT BY DAY, WEEK OR MONTH* was lettered in black against a dusty white signboard. Above it Miyako Hotel winked its neon red off and on. Built around a recessed courtyard, it had seen better days. Its office niche, dark and woody, was tended by a bespectacled, thin, tired-looking clerk with shirtsleeves hiked by rubber bands. He was backed by a wood honeycomb of numerous mail slots. Outside the office sat a Japanese newspaper stand. To left of the main entrance was a tobacco shop run by an elderly couple. To right was Sato's barbershop which, by its location, offered a guaranteed hotel clientele. It also housed them, daughter and father, in one of the Miyako's cheaper, dark apartments facing the alley. Perhaps early on her mother had complained of the cramped quarters but Michie scarcely recalled this fretting. After three years battling pleurisy, her mother died, leaving father and daughter to maintain their meager lives, spare on leisure and long on toil. The shop held their all: dreams as well as day to day living.

Promptly at eight o'clock, six mornings a week, Sato-*san* and Michie opened up the business. Often, even at this early hour, slouched next to the peppermint striped pole affixed to right of the entrance, were two anxious men, their shaggy hair badly in need of trimming.

"Gooda morning," Sato greeted them in his immaculate white tunic. From his hair parted like a furrowed field, to his spit polished black shoes, he was fastidiously groomed. The faint antiseptic smell of Listerine followed him.

The first two customers occupied chairs with split, padded, shiny, plastic seats lined against the wall. A table of newspapers and magazines sat to right of a glass cabinet crammed with colored bottles of varied hair tonics, some looking curiously like vinegar cruets, their emerald and aqua dazzled by morning sunlight. Midway through the room, four leather and steel chairs faced the wall with mirrors on either side. The floor was clean with a black and white checked linoleum echoing black and white tiles above two deep sinks. Next to a towel rack hinged to a white, plastered wall, stood a straw broom. Above it hung a calender featuring Mt. Fuji and cherry trees.

Sato-*san* stood behind a chair and beckoned one of the men. A white sheet cape in his left hand quickly was whisked around this customer's neck and fastened with a firm bow. Kleenex was tucked in between neck and sheet.

"Cut short," said the man, squirming into the padded seat. He flashed a smile revealing two missing front teeth; the rest were tea-stained.

"Hi, hi," grunted an obliging Sato-*san*, casting a circumspect glance at the head before him. With scissors and comb in his small, stubby fingers, he deftly cut away chunks of black hair. Since Sato was a quiet man and the customer, also close-mouthed, there was total silence between them.

Meanwhile, Michie, also in a white tunic, hers over a dull mustard green dress, looked to the other customer with a professional stare. She motioned to the seat. The man responded, plopping himself brusquely into the chair. With a slip of the wrist, she snapped a sheet around his neck as he studied her. She had a strong-willed look about her and hands that were wiry and firm. A half smile flicked on her face nervously as she asked the man how he wanted his hair cut. That she was competent, there was no doubt once the cutting began. Her every movement was quick and flowing as she clipped with comb in her hand. Convinced that she knew her business, the man closed his eyes.

On a typical day, within the hour three more customers entered through the screen door. One, an old-timer, shouted "Sato-*san*!" waving a folded *Asashi Shimbun* newspaper in the air. Michie stole a shy glance his way, merely to confirm the familiar voice.

The shop hummed with the finishing buzz of an electric clipper. Between jobs, Michie swept cuttings into a pile before a large, metal trash can. Clanks of a tonic bottle signaled the final dab of hair dressing. Carefully removing the protective sheet, she brushed off hair from the man's neck with a soft-bristled brush. At this moment, she smiled while he stole a furtive glance at himself in the mirror. By noon the shop smelled a combination of pomade, talc, shaving cream and vaseline. At twelve noon, Michie left for a quick lunch at the corner noodle shop. Upon her return, her father grabbed his lunch at either the Miyako Restaurant or the Ebesu Inn in the next block.

Choice customers came in for both shave and a haircut. Al Afook, Miyako's sole Chinese boarder, was just such a man. Reckoned as a heavy tipper, he was on Michie's "regular" list. In fact, he brazenly displayed his preference for her service. This attention was not lost to Sato-*san* who, in spare but cogent remarks to his daughter made clear his displeasure. One particular instance during the war stayed with her. It was a time when "due to the Emergency" wealthy households let go their Japanese maids and gardeners; businesses dismissed them for "public relations reasons;" in military installations, "for security reasons." Al Alfook was exceptional in his loyalty. Moreover, in a time when nylon hosiery was scarce, thanks to a need for nylon parachutes, Al had offered "I can get nylons for you. Just let me know how many you need."

Flustered but secretly pleased by his offer, Michie had told her father of Al's generous proposition.

"What he want from you? You no think about that?" came his seething retort, the reason why she wore thick rayons until after the war. Nonetheless, she did not foget Al's consideration.

Between the unemployed who sauntered in leisurely and the bustling businessmen who darted in and waited glancing at their wrist watches every twenty minutes, children sent in after school with exact change pinned into their pockets, the customer stream was constant. Many had been faithful, going back to their childhood days. Sato-*san*'s memory, in this respect, was a calender of the town's Japanese population. Occasionally, whites, Hawaiians, Chinese or Filipinos entered the shop but they were the exception and Sato-*san* dealt with them on a strictly pay-cash basis, reserving charge accounts for a favored few.

Her face revealing neither enthusiasm nor disgust with her task, Michie had helped her father on a full-time basis since she graduated from high school. But in fact, while only an eighth grader, she had hung around the shop after school hours to keep a sharp eye on his method of work. Sweeping and dusting had been her responsibility those days, Sometimes she would be allowed to hold up a mirror for customers to preen themselves. After this, they would slip coins into her hand, eliciting smiles from Michie and a fatherly snort from Sato-*san*.

When she was older, he allowed her to cut his own thinning hair as training for the day when she would work full time. That she would follow her father's trade arose as a taken-for-granted fact. There was never need to discuss the matter. She liked everything about the shop. In general, Michie discussed little with him; the gap of age and sex was too wide to overstep the bounds of mutual respect. If only she had a mother or sister to talk to. It was the only thing she regretted.

That Michie too would be a barber was a part of her heritage she accepted. As a child she vaguely remembered her mother speaking of a blind aunt in Japan who worked as a shampooer. The tradition was there, something to do with hair. She felt if her mother were alive, she would approve.

"When Michie goin work?" customers had asked of Sato-*san*.

"Little bit more," he answered with his usual verbal parsimony. Michie met his eyes with a dutiful daughter glance. Sato closed the matter with a clearing of his throat, stropping a long razor blade with sidewise swipes that whistled.

✳ ✳ ✳

From early on in her apprenticeship, Michie's presence cast a subtle, atmospheric difference in the shop. Sato himself sensed that whereas a once-a-month customer formerly waited until he could no longer stand his shaggy hair, there grew an increased number since Michie who frequented the business within a week's time. Discounting womanizers and gay blades, this curious phenomenon surfaced among former slobs. Too, Sato noted that they would line up specifically for Michie's service. Passing attention would engender a slight lift of Sato's lips, but when a man's overtures became too obvious, Sato set down a heavy foot. Such was the case when Toru Ozaki, a swarthy man with bushy eyebrows, made himself so conspicuous by his over-generous tips that she declared "Toru must be doing okay at his job to have so much money, eh?" "Toru work with pigs and horses. In Japan, only outcasts do that kind of work," said Sato, leaving no doubt that she was not to encourage Toru.

On another instance she would never forget, he cut down another suitor with "Man like that will give you kids with curly hair, dark skin and big eyes just like him got!". His tone of voice alone hinted disparagement not lost on Michie.

Of her admirers throughout the years, none was more persistent than Shigeru Ishida, a high school classmate. He had been attracted to her since "homeroom" days together where they sat across a table and she helped him with algebra. Too shy to walk home with her after school, he nonetheless lagged behind to keep an eye on her. After graduation, Shigeru, still afflicted with extreme timorousness, worked as clerk in his father's hardware store, and although they lived miles outside Lunalilo, he always had his hair cut at Sato's shop, where Michie greeted him with scant remarks he went home to repeat to himself.

※ ※ ※

Years passed. Soon most of Michie's classmates were married and of those not wedded or engaged, parents grew anxious. If Sato worried about her singleness, he did not indicate his concern. Together they carried the burden of the business as though work were the only thing in their lives. Sundays, her only day off, was spent washing, ironing or mending. One day Michie studied herself carefully in a mirror, noting her lackluster complexion and a listlessness in her eyes she had associated with old ladies, an opacity seen in inanimate objects such as stones on a seashore. Now she feared she too had become one of those dull stones. Within a week, she learned from another classmate she happened to meet at the noodle shop that Shigeru was dating Hatsue Yamada, a girl from the other side of the island. From this same friend, she learned that the Ishida family had carefully considered the obstacles to a Sato-Ishida marriage. Because Michie was an only child, Sato had voiced his wish to have whoever married her take on the Sato name. Of course, as is usual under the circumstance, only a poor man would accede to this request. The Ishidas were not poor; they owned a thriving business. There was even talk of opening up another hardware store across town.

Too, there was the matter of Michie's occupation. Barbering was looked upon as a job without dignity. Not only was the matter of hair degrading, but there was also the unseemly fact that she dealt largely with male customers. A good girl from a good family would never stoop to such a profession. It was only a step below bartender. Considering all particulars, a marriage to Hatsue would be more amenable to everyone concerned.

The next time Shigeru came to the shop, Michie appeared sullen.

He sensed a strain in the way she said "Back again?". His attempt at small talk was rebuffed with a pinch of her lip. Most of the time, she averted her head.

How could he come here, of all places, she asked herself now that the *yuino*, the binding gift had already been exchanged between Yamadas and Ishidas? After such a declaration, tantamount to law, neither party could withdraw without losing face.

Her father too must have sensed his daughter's unhappiness, for three months later, Michie received a letter from her aunt Katsu Oyama, a sister on her mother's side, living in Hanapepe. In the note, the elderly relative had suggested that Michie come to apprentice in her husband's bakery shop, famed for its black bean *manju* rolls. Delicately she had hinted that Michie might make new friends her own age in their rural town. Surely her mother would have approved of this move. But the aunt did not surmise her niece's stubborn loyalty to her father. "We too busy," Michie had said, reneging the invitation.

❈ ❈ ❈

Ever busy, Sato-san worked until the day he died of a heart attack. Circumstances changed rapidly after that. Long time owners of the Miyako were replaced by Zenko Doi, an enterprising bachelor from California who wore black vests and slicked his hair down to a cowlick. A small, neat bristle of a gray moustache lined the thin upper lip of this man known for his absurd punctiliousness.

Most surprisingly, shortly after her father's death, Michie married the Chinese Al Afook. They continued to live at the Miyako and had two sons named Wilfred and Bruce. Amply supported by Al's bookkeeping salary, Michie no longer felt chained to the barber business. Consequently, she sold her father's shop to the Tachibana brothers who brought with them an entirely new clientele of young men demanding that no clippers be used on their hair. They preferred it styled long! Still barbering on a part-time basis for the new owners, Michie seemed content with the change. "Everything just fine," she remarked to old customers who asked.

Frank and Don Tachibana handled the young crowd. Michie clipped the elderly. They appreciated her soft touch and silence. They don't make them like that no more, they said of her.

LEARNING

Hawaii, 1933

IT DID NOT MATTER that they hadn't seen it. The three girls had devoured enough data from glossy magazines about the movie that as far as they were concerned, the popcorn had already been digested and they had as good as seen it.

"I hear she runs nude through the woods."

"I thought she swam naked in a pool."

"Wasn't it a bathtub scene?"

"Everyone's talking about 'Ecstasy.'"

"Especially about Heddy Lamarr."

"It's really something."

During their senior year, the three girls had been the best of friends. Now each would go her separate way. Eileen and Myro looked forward to the university in September but Shizuko Hata said she wanted a permanent job. Distinguished in high school for her cuteness as head pom pom girl and attendant to the Senior Prom Queen, Shiz preened herself before a mirror. It was in preparation for a job interview. Carefully she outlined lips with carmine Tangee and re-arranged spit curls for that Flapper Fanny look. A final glance at the mirror, a tug at her skirt and she was ready.

"Job hunting?" her mother asked, entering the room.

"Yeah, I have the ad somewhere here." She rummaged through her lauhala purse for a crumpled piece of newspaper. "Kinda strange

63

sounding but interesting I think. Listen to this: 'Wanted, artistic type girl for design work,'" she read.

"Sounds like you."

"I thought so too."

"Well, see how it is."

"That's what I'm going to do. See you."

She repeated to herself the address then hurried to catch the bus. Located next to a car repair shop, in a semi-residential section of town, her goal was a warehouse fronted with a Palmer Enterprises sign. She entered the door marked Office.

A middle-aged man of average height, garbed casually in seersucker suit and polo shirt, rose to meet her. She noticed his slight paunch, dark curly hair and pleasant though ruddy face. Typical *haole* type, she thought to herself.

"I came to see about the job you advertised — artistic girl?"

"Sure, sit down." He eyed her thoroughly, up and down. He spoke in a relaxed way, leaning against the filing cabinet, fingering a cigarette in a hairy hand. "My name is Palmer, Ron Palmer. And yours is Miss — ?"

The hand he offered was warm. "Shizuko Hata. People call me Shiz for short."

"Okay, Shiz, now let me tell you something about the job. . . ." He went on to elaborate details entailed in the position, the particulars of which she concluded she could handle easily enough. After the introduction, he took her through the plant where she saw five workers silk-screening bolts of fabric with Hawaiian motifs such as breadfruit leaves, bird of paradise, surfers and so on. The usual stuff. Creating such designs would be her job.

While Mr. Palmer introduced the work crew, she felt an undercurrent of snide glances as though the likes of her were an all too familiar parade to the staff. Their stares gave her unease. It was certainly not Mr. Palmer's fault. On the contrary, he attempted to put them at ease with a limp joke about sleeping on and off the job, a joke greeted with snickers.

She was relieved to return to the privacy of Mr. Palmer's office. Consulting his watch, he asked "Did you bring your lunch?"

"No, I didn't expect to stay here all day."

"Okay, how about lunch with me?" It was his tone, as easy as turning on the tap. This was something he did every day. He was cool. She too would be cool. "Okay," she said.

Cupping her elbow, he guided her to his car, a Victoria Brougham, she remembered, baby blue enamel. Opening the door, he helped her into its beige leather seat. The fluid suavity of his conduct continued throughout lunch.

Fisherman's Lounge where they dined was a place she'd known only by sight. While riding the bus, she had passed its oversized neon sign. Its parking lot jammed with fancy cars. Popular with executives, at noon it bulged with businessmen, dark-suited professionals sipping martinis with clientele, secretary or an occasional wife. Seated at one of its spotlessly linened tables, beneath a hanging philodendron, she felt that she didn't belong here. She was not like one of those be-jeweled women, toying with their cocktail glasses and laughing easily.

Mr. Palmer, on the other hand, seemed to be swimming in his element. Backround Hawaiian music, a blend of lethargic velveteen voices and steel guitars made him happy. His fingers kept drumming to its lazy beat. A waiter came to their table with menus. After a close study, reading even the fine print, Mr. Palmer asked "Now then, what'll you have? Any preferences?"

"I'll have whatever you suggest," she said, conscious of the waiter's eyes upon her. The air conditioning chilled her.

"Is there a house special?" Mr. Palmer asked the waiter.

"Sir, I would recommend the Parker Ranch beef today," said the waiter.

"Fine, we'll try it. I'll also have a bloody Mary just for kicks." He winked.

Leaning back in her chair, Shiz observed Mr. Palmer's cigarette choreography: thumping each against a shiny, gold monogrammed case, snapping a lighter, flicking ashes precisely into an ashtray so that a ruby eye of his gold ring flashed. "Now then, tell me about yourself, Shiz. Have you any hobbies?" he asked. He narrowed his eyes, which were a smoky gray.

"Well, I like to go to the movies a lot and I collect matchbook covers."

"You paint or draw in your spare time, I suppose?"

"Yes, I took a class at the Academy last summer that taught me how to draw things music inspires." She wondered if all this was kid stuff to him.

"Really?" He leaned back in his seat, squinting his eyes as if to snap a photograph of her. "That's very interesting. Abstract things?"

"Not always. Sometimes I see people or certain lines, flowers and things like that in the music. It depends." (Art interested him. She liked that.)

"Uh-huh." He hunched over, elbows propped on the table, hands clasped under his chin, re-garnering all his attention on her. Shiz nibbled at pebble-sized bits of steak and potatoes while talk rambled on about beach-wear and towels. Finally, the last course was served and consumed.

"Through with dessert?"

"Yes, the mango ice cream was delicious."

"Come on. Let's get out of here."

"Thanks for the lunch, Mr. Palmer."

"It was my pleasure," he said, assisting her out of the chair.

* * *

Leaving Fisherman's Lounge, Mr. Palmer drove down King Street to the banking district for an appointment he had with a shipping company. Shiz, meanwhile, waited for him in the car. When Mr. Palmer returned, he told her "Those people were real nice to me. Who says they have a stranglehold on the islands? They were real nice people."

His words meant nothing to her but she replied, "That's good," which seemed to satisfy him because he flashed another easy smile at her. It made him look handsome. He *is* a nice, generous man she thought as he asked her if the wind through the open windows bothered her. Considerate too.

"About your salary, Shiz, I think you'll find me a generous man. Giving bonuses for good work is how I keep my crew happy. You can ask them." Again he flashed that radiant smile. "I want you to be happy," he said patting her knee lightly.

They continued driving, not back to the office as she had expected but instead to the Waikiki district, onto a side street where sleek apartment buildings towered between palms bereft of coconuts. Parking the car in a private garage, he asked "Do you mind if I pick up some papers in my apartment?"

"No," she answered.

"Come with me then."

She followed him, entering a glass-fronted building where a doorman in red uniform said "Gooday, Mr. Palmer." With hand on her forearm, he led her through a foyer where they took a silent, carpeted elevator to the second floor and his apartment. Once inside its soundproof seclusion, he excused himself to change. He returned wearing a Hawaiian floral shirt and loose trousers. She was taken aback by the difference clothes made in this instance. He looked to her like one of the ubiquitous *haole* tourists she saw strolling the beachwalks any evening, prowling for quick pick-ups. She sat somewhat tensely on the edge of a chair close to the entranceway.

Again he left the room. She heard the slam of a refrigerator door. Ice cubes clinked.

Heaving a sigh, he flopped himself into a reclining, black leather chair. slipped off his shoes, and propped his stockinged feet onto a footstool. "Now then," he said, sipping a drink, "Let's talk about the movies. You said you see a lot of them?"

"Yes, I do."

"Well then, are you up on the latest?"

"I think so."

"Have you seen 'Ecstasy'?"

"Yes," she blurted out before she could catch herself.

"What did you think about it?"

"Oh, it's a terrific movie all right," she continued the lie.

With a tiny stick he swirled ice cubes. "You think so, huh?"

"Everyone says so." She tried to sound casual.

"Come here, Shiz." He beckoned her with a crooked finger. "Come over here by me and I'll show you some *real* ecstasy."

Hearing this, the girl grabbed her purse and ran out the door they'd entered. She did it with such exigent speed that Mr. Palmer, groggy at the time, did not lift himself out of his chair. Her sudden dash had caught him by surprise.

She ran to the elevator. Drats, it was occupied. She tore open the exit door and scurried down stairs to the ground floor, past the doorman and into the harsh, sweet afternoon light of day. Luckily the Waihio bus pulled in just as she reached the corner. Quickly she boarded it and sat in back near the rear exit. She felt her heart continue to race. Steady, she told herself, you're safe now. You managed to escape. You're okay. She looked out the window seeing people carry on their humdrum lives as usual but she was not the same. She felt innocence race past her as swiftly as the day's traffic.

THE RING

Overlooking Waikiki, Diamond Head and Honolulu, there is a hilltop called Punchbowl because of its roundish shape. It is a veteran's cemetery, a serene, grassy place lined with plumeria trees and flat gray markers. Picnics, weddings and christenings take place in small, private ceremonies as family members attempt to revive their ties to one now dead.

Among the faithful is a slight woman who always comes with a small bouquet in hand of mock oranges, bridal wreath or gardenias, flowers from her own garden. On her finger she wears two rings, one a gold band, and the other, a tarnished class ring. Her name is Fumi.

An island girl of immigrant parents, she blended into colors of her school class the way a water-colorist bleeds his palette. Back before the war, she was in many ways, typical. Barely five feet tall, she was the shortest senior, this despite the fact that both her parents were above average height for Japanese. "Just like your auntie Shizu in Japan," her mother explained. "That sister never reached my shoulders even with high heels. That's the truth." Her matter of fact comment settled the subject for Fumi who, in her mind, envisioned a dumpy, kimono-clad lady somewhere in Japan, poised under a pink-blossomed cherry tree, umbrella in hand, the source of her own runt inheritance.

She did not mind so much the *idea* of being small. What she resented was the way people, always with kind intentions, paired you with a twin. If you were skinny and tall, they suggested partnership with someone skinny and tall. If you were short and fat, again they paired you accordingly as though life was a constant search for your mirror image.

Hints might drop out of the blue from a best friend as well as a casual acquaintance. Just yesterday, Sadako had asked Fumi, "Ever notice that Marumoto boy?" Then followed an unsolicited suggestion for whom she might date: "He's short just like you!" So when Fumi first met Hisashi "Stumpy" Marumoto at that Saturday night YWCA dance, they were practically shoved together for the opening Artie Shaw "Begin the Beguine" fox trot. As expected, the tall pairs clicked off like a military drill followed by those of average height until it seemed to Fumi that only midgets remained gaping at each other, asking, "Shall we?"

What she noticed immediately about Hisashi making his way toward her, was his nervous smile and a habit of running his hand over his belt buckle as though checking to see that his trousers had not fallen off. The other, nicer thing about Hisashi was his very pleasant low tone of voice, the nearest thing to Claude Raines, a Hollywood favorite with Fumi.

After "May I have this dance?" pronounced firmly and to the point, she felt his right hand touching her waist, his left hand clasping her right hand, a proper distance of six inches between them. She was pleased to find that his hands were not clammy. Instead they felt warm yet dry as he danced confidently to the insistent moan of Harry James' trumpet, whirling her around the dance floor, sluicing through couples like guiding a boat. The first thing he said was "My name's Hisashi." His eyes were on the same level as hers.

"Mine's Fumi," was her timorous reply. Fumi herself was surprised at her hesitation. How to explain it? She thought it was Hisashi's confidence, the way he seemed to have everything under his control. In contrast, Fumi felt jittery, fearful of being swept away by the big band's hypnotic music filling the warm, Saturday-night, gymnasium air with romance, Saturday-night romance. Was everyone else on the floor eyeing them, two shorties? A starched seam of her dress where his hand embraced her felt stiff, pressed into the flesh of her back.

"Where do you work?" he asked, between spins.

"At the plantation store. Sales."

"Near home?"

"Yes, we live near the Nalihi plantation. And you?"

"Oh, I'm working at my brother-in-law's shoe store. But it's only temporary."

"Temporary?"

"Yeah, I'm thinking of enlisting."

"The army?"

"Like everybody else. Already I know three buddies who signed up. I don't want to be left behind."

Curdled emotions about the war left her speechless. What could she say? She was relieved to hear him continue the conversation.

"Naturally, my folks don't like the idea. . .the oldest boy and all. . . . Still I can't just sit around and since the war, Japs like me can't get jobs."

"The war. . .yeah, I know." She left the subject dangling. She didn't want to talk about the war with the Japs when they themselves were Japs. Now — together — they were dancing to all-American pop music. What did the war have to do with them? For the remainder of the number he was silent. Strange how she found him growing taller in her mind. When the music stopped, he escorted her back to one of the metal chairs aligning the wall. "Save the last dance for me, okay?" he asked.

"Sure thing," said Fumi, fully realizing the import of his request, a canon among partners that the last dance was reserved for sweethearts. Did she do the right thing? She had to admit she liked him and yes, she wanted to see more of Stumpy.

❊ ❊ ❊

On their first date they attended a Katharine Hepburn-Spencer Tracy matinee. They even bought popcorn, placing the bag atop their gas masks (G.I. issue, a requirement of all civilians). If Hepburn in heels towered over Tracy, it did not bother Fumi. She liked that less than Hollywood ideal.

Thereafter, Hisashi lost no time in pursuit of Fumi. An understanding evolved that he would be her steady with a corner on all her free time. Curfew and blackouts restricted them to daytime activities such as beach strolls, guava picking or just chewing the fat on the front veranda. Slowly Hisashi opened up, talking about issues really important to him. For the first time in his life he found himself divulging feelings toward his family members. Small talk, usually a bore, became exciting. Fumi made the difference; she listened to him.

"He's a good boy," her father remarked of Hisashi the first time the young man called for her. What had impressed him was the way Hisashi, without being questioned, offered backround information that seemed important to him: "My father works at Kuhio Savings &Loan downtown. We're Yamaguchi *ken* folks. Two boys in the family, my brother is a landscape architect, did the Queen Emma Hotel in Waikiki, fancy beach place with travelers palms in front. Mom, she just stays home, sometimes does *sumi-e*." He even mentioned what high school he attended. Unlike some of the smart aleck younger ones, this boy was brought up right; he respected older folk. He had good manners; he bowed. What's more, his Japanese was surprisingly good.

From the onset, Fumi and Hisashi were a twosome Made for Each Other friends claimed. Informal meals with Fumi's family was a standing invitation, always followed by front porch talks, the only place where they had privacy.

Too soon the day for Hisashi to volunteer came. As a green army recruit, part of the 442nd combat regiment, a special unit consisting of Island and Mainland volunteers, Hisashi felt at home with buddies he knew. In fact it seemed like homecoming with all his classmates enlisting too.

Before Hisashi's departure, Fumi was invited to a private family dinner. It was on this last occasion that he gave her the ring, his class ring, a thick silver-plated one with Lunalilo High engraved inside. Strapped for money at the time, he had bought the cheaper version instead of the expensive one with a stone. Now he regretted his choice. Fumi, doubtless, would have liked the colored birthstone. But she understood. "Due to the emergency" she explained, a phrase tacked onto anything to be deferred. Later on, after the entire business of war was over, he'd buy a real diamond sparkler. He swore it and she knew he meant it.

She continued to work as usual at the plantation store. Co-workers, knowing that she was practically engaged to Hisashi, asked from time to time how he liked the army. "He's fine," she'd answer, always a little shyly.

One day she received this APO letter, the first from him:

Dear Fumi:
You should see me now in my short GI haircut and GI everything. Boy the army had one heck of a time fitting us midget guys. So many of us from Hawaii are runts, you know. Ha. Ha. As time goes by, life is getting better. (I hope.) The food is okay but I miss my mom's cooking, natch. Sure would like to go to a Saturday nite dance again. We hear the old songs on the Hit Parade. The guys and I, when we get together always end up talking about old times. Sure miss you and promise to make up for lost time when we get back. In the meantime, all talk is about going overseas. "Take good care of yourself" as the song goes. "You belong to me," And how!

Love you,
Hisashi

Fumi read and re-read the letter so many times, the tissue-thin paper on which it was written grew frail. It was followed by other letters, some dealing with basic training in a southern camp. Later, letters came from overseas, always vague about the exact locale but emphatic on combat somewhere in the rough mountain terrain of Italy where they met action.

Dear Fumi:

I am writing this letter on top of my bunk bed. There is a poker game going on and things are getting noisy. You know us *Kanakas* (Hawaiians), we play all the time. Ha Ha. Thanks for the last photos you sent. You sure look nice, just like I remember you.

Things are getting rough due to the damn war. Lost some good buddies. It ain't easy. Will tell you more about it some day when I'm back home. Right now, I'd rather forget. Give my regards to your folks and drop in to see my mom anytime. She says she likes you.

Tats Ushida says he knows your sister, met her at the armory dance. Small world, isn't it? One barracks buddy has a uke. Hearing him play sure makes me homesick.

That's about it for now. "Goodnight Sweetheart, till we meet tomorrow," as the song goes. Save me the last dance.

Love you,
Hisashi

It was the last letter she would receive from him.

❋ ❋ ❋

The day she received a phone call from his father she guessed immediately that it would be urgent. "Just come to our place. We have something to talk over." It had overtones of dread.

She was right. A grave-looking Marumoto-san met her at the front door. He was a ruddy complexioned man with bushy eyebrows, giving him a constant scowl. But Fumi, as she got to know him better, discovered he was a gentle, considerate man, belying his stern appearance. Mrs. Marumoto took her place beside him like a shadow, her face bloated with tears, averted as she sobbed. Fumi placed a hand on the lady's heaving shoulders.

Once seated in the family's living room, Marumoto said "Hisashi died, Fumi-*chan*. We just heard from the Army." Despite the fact that she had steeled herself for just such a possibility, when it came, the shock of hearing the awful words stunned. She shuddered at the impact. Nothing. Now Hisashi was gone. Pulling herself together, she managed to comfort Mrs. Marumoto while Mr. Marumoto, a man who could not cry, remained expressionless.

⁎ ⁎ ⁎

For a long time Fumi did not cry either. She told herself that both she and Stumpy knew that they would have to wait out an uncertain "duration" during which anything could happen. And just as she had seen her own parents stoically accept bad luck along with the good, she told herself "It can't be helped," as Fumi calmly accepted a future with only memories of her wartime romance.

Now, many years later, she still visits Punchbowl with the flowers. You may see her standing quietly, the one with the kerchief on her head when it is windy. Sometimes it is very windy up here.

A GAME OF CHERRY BLOSSOMS

As far back as Kimiko Shimada could remember, there had always been her father's Saturday night card games. Not even his own father's funeral could have taken precedence. Arrangements were made for an afternoon memorial service and cremation at four o'clock, leaving Mr. Shimada's evening free for business as usual, which is how he referred half-jokingly to his weekly meetings. The rest of the family knew better. His pre-occupation with cards became an obsession. Calendar entrenched as her mother's weekly temple visits, these all-male gatherings for a game of *sakura* furnished for him a close-knit coterie. Whether its members played *sakura* for his friendship or only *sakura* players were considered his friends, it was not easy to sort out. The fact remained that the pastime took on supreme importance, shaping their lives in a silent, invidious way.

A bookkeeper by trade, Shimada-*san* was a hefty man of above-average height, brusque in manner and speech. To his obliging wisp of a wife and his daughters, he rumbled orders, criticism and opinion which hung in midair as sacred and immutable.

They were a family of five girls. Kimiko and her sisters Fusai, Ikuko and little Hisako. The eldest daughter Tamiyo was married to a blacksmith's son who, through negotiations of a mediator, had agreed to assume the Shimada name since they were without a male heir. As Tamiyo's husband, he was obliged, of course, to attend the games while she remained at home to care for their three young children.

After Tamiyo left home, the task of greeting and serving the

Saturday visitors became Kimiko's prime responsibility with her mother playing a secondary kitchen role throughout the evening.

And exactly what was the game to which Shimada-*san* was addicted? Small enough to fit into the palm of one's hand, *sakura* cards are stubby, thick and ebony, depicting colorful plants, animals, and of course, cherry blossoms, the name card. Slammed against a tabletop, they clap like wooden rice paddles. Through a thin wall separating her bedroom from the gathering, Kimiko would hear these card slams in cleaver cadence against Japanese talk, a drone of grunts and hisses saturating the late hours.

Neighbors knew Saturday eves by the din emanating from Shimada windows. Like ocean waves guffaw would be followed by quiet only to swell again to boisterousness. The cycle persisted into early morning when finally the house would be laid to rest.

Horrid Saturday nights — Kimiko hated them. With the tortoise cat Neko settled at the foot of her bed, she fought the disturbance, but sleep would be difficult. Burying her head in quilted bedding, she hoped to shut out noise but nothing worked. Only after hours of fitful toss and turning, her body aching with exhaustion, sleep would finally overcome her. It was the same for all members of the household.

Among the *sakura* players welcomed to their home throughout the years was a man known to her as Hino-*san*. A bookkeeper like her father, he had the build of a *sumo* wrestler, bloated with swollen flesh, his face like a mass of bee stings with the narrowest slits for eyes. His coarse hair which she imagined to be like needles to the touch, bristled from stretched pores. Fastidiously clean, a man of two baths per day, yet his clothes clung to him with moistness and his hands, unusually small for a man his size, felt like wet towels. A nervous smile like an involuntary tic accompanied everything he said, so that it was a puzzle to figure out exactly what his real feelings were. This uncertainty made people distrust the man, for who could smile forever and mean every minute of it? As with a crocodile, it was easier to be on guard with Hino-*san*.

On Kimiko, even as a little girl, he heaped sugary attention: red coconut balls, peanut brittle, caramels or Black Jack gum. Warmed by the heat of his sweaty palms, the treats would drop limp into Kimiko's hands, their cellophane wrappers stuck fast to the contents. If on occasion his pockets were empty of goodies, he would immediately run to the nearest grocery store to remedy the oversight. Sweets in hand, Hino unfailingly followed an elaborate ritual, presenting the gifts and then waiting, still smiling, for her thanks. Kimiko's gratitude, however mechanical, filled him with exaggerated pleasure. Once or twice she noticed moisture in his eyes while he awaited her one or two words of appreciation.

As she grew older and declined the treats, saying they were bad for her teeth, a wounded Hino would press them into her hands, explaining that he had no use for them. These incidents proved to be more and more awkward for a maturing Kimiko. Transformed like a butterfly from a cocoon, the once thin, small-boned child grew into a lovely girl with pleasant, tidy features. Early on she exhibited a flair for silk embroidering, a penchant handed down from her mother's side. A quick learner, she did well in school and made friends easily. Takamine-*san*, one of her father's close friends and a longtime card player who owned a bakery, gave her an after school job sweeping up the shop and washing dishes. Assiduously she saved every penny she earned in a bank account so that by her senior year she had accumulated $362.37 — a lot of money. Suddenly her blossoming awakened the interests of the town's eligible bachelors, foremost among them Hino-*san*.

But Kimiko loathed the man. While her parents and younger sisters treated him as one would a circus bear, a burly animal with a repertoire of tricks, for Kimiko he aroused only disdain. Instances when she and her mother made preparation for the parlor games, they closed all the room's windows and slatted down all venetian blinds, sparing the neighbors the weekly din. During the games, it was her job to refill bowls of rice crackers, empty ashtrays or re-heat porcelain *sake* containers. At various times, elephantine Hino would corner her. Pinned against a wall, she would feel heat radiating from his body, see eyes locked into small folds, rings around his neck, cheeks glistening with the ruddiness of ripe pomegranate. She shuddered, bumping into the blubbery flesh of his elbow.

But the foremost reason for her aversion was an incident which occurred when she was five years old, yet the memory of it remained indelible.

One evening, after the opening round, excessive with money and over-indulgence of *sake*, a drunken Hino stumbled from the parlor, bracing his large frame against the hallway wall to keep from falling. Kimiko, awakened by bangs of his clumsy lunges against a loosened floor mat, peeked out from a crack of her door. At that moment, Neko darted out from her room, entangling itself under Hino's feet. To her horror, she saw him kick the animal with his foot. Hurled across the entire length of the hallway, the cat landed with a dull thud against the kitchen door. He laughed as the injured animal limped away.

He had laughed. She had witnessed something which years later still smarted, altering her estimate of him forever. From that turning point, whenever he frequented their home, although she displayed her usual courtesy, she no longer considered him a friend.

So her family did not understand, twelve years later, why she refused his offer of marriage. The man was practically a member of the family, so loyally had he attended all card games despite illness or inconvenience to himself. To every request of Mrs. Shimada, whether it was pounding rice cakes, a holiday ritual for creating the traditional black bean patties, or purchasing a choice red snapper for the New Year's celebration, he had hopped to the favor. And hadn't he shown extreme patience, waiting the years for Kimiko to grow up? "*Baka*" townswomen said of her denial. She was crazy not to accept his offer. That he would be an exemplary provider was unquestionable. Besides, he was neat and clean. What more could a girl want?

Still Kimiko balked. Her rejection at first aroused a curiously mild reproach from her father. Expecting thunder, the family met an unnerving calm. A man of Hino's patience can wait for tides to change, he hinted with a card player's fatalistic optimism.

At the following week's card game, Hino was conspicuously absent. His omission affronted Shimada-*san* personally. Was he ill? A terrible accident? No? What then? Mrs. Shimada was sent to Hino's apartment. The landlady said she didn't know anything.

Mr. Shimada instructed his wife to prepare a gift of Hino's favorite, a platter of rice cakes sweetened with mashed white beans. The goodies, artistically arranged on a red lacquer tray, decorated with a sprig of maiden-hair fern, would be taken by Kimiko. Further, her father requested that she wear a certain kimono, one with pink rosebuds which Hino favored.

When informed of the proposal, she balked. So adamant was her refusal, her mother was shocked. Never before had the girl displayed such effrontery. Not to comply with her father's wishes? Unthinkable!

"She says she doesn't like him," her mother reported.

"What? An old friend like him? Nonsense!"

"I don't know why she refuses, so stubborn."

"She is a child acting childishly. Tell her that!"

Alone with her mother, she listened but said nothing.

"*Otosan* (father) is only thinking about your welfare you know," Mrs. Shimada said. The natural alliance of two women against male tyranny made it difficult for her to defend him. She understood Kimiko's obstinacy too well. As a girl in Japan, she too had refused a suitor pressed on her by her parents. She too had defied them. Yet she continued, "He thinks Hino will be best husband for you. Try to understand. We talk more tomorrow."

Closeting her feelings, the girl retreated to her room where for hours she stared glassy-eyed out the window, listening to the wind, noting the suppleness of her neighbor's bamboo as it bent sidewise with each gust. Neko sidled up and rubbed its nose against her feet.

It was Mrs. Shimada who delivered the rice cakes to Hino.

✳ ✳ ✳

Early the next morning, Mrs. Shimada discovered the empty bed. Kimiko had fled.

"*Baka*! The girl is crazy leaving home like that!" shouted Shimada-*san* in a voice which made his wife cringe into a little ball. Trembling with shame and dismay, she absorbed her daughter's misdeed as though it were a wart on her own skin.

His rage festered. "The girl is crazy! Where could she go? Did she have money?" Bloated, his face darkened to a blood purple.

"She had saved money from her work at the bakery shop. She's a hard working girl."

Shimada-*san* ground his teeth and slapped his right hand against his upper left arm. The clap thudded deep inside Mrs. Shimada as she stood cowering.

Then she went to the kitchen and began to prepare breakfast. Her hands, long the capable implement of women's work, moved through memorized motions while she thought of Kimiko. In tense silence the two ate orange slices, toast and soft boiled eggs. After Shimada drank two cups of coffee, he lit a Lucky Strike with a house match, sucking in air as though gasping for breath. A gray funnel of smoke much like the last traces of a steam locomotive dissipated in the early dawn chill.

He spoke calmly, "Next week you better show Fusai how to warm up the *sake*. Yoshimi-*san* is coming to play."

ONE MORNING

Two OLD LADIES, neighbors across a chicken wire fence, were hanging up wash in their back yards when it happened. CRASH BANG splintered the morning air.

"What dat?" asked Conchita, slightly fatter of the two, taking a clothespin out of her mouth and slipping it into her apron pocket.

The skinnier one called Kaz, short for Kazuko, froze, still holding onto a towel on her left hand.

Both ladies had gray hair and skin brown as potatoes. Simultaneously they turned heads toward the alley. "Accident for sure, eh?" Conchita blurted.

"Bust up car sound like."

"We go see for make sure," said Conchita, leaving a sheet dangling on the clothesline.

At the far end of the alleyway they saw a car with its front end squashed against a coconut tree. The crunch looked bad: one fender was folded back like an accordion, headlight gone, windshield crazed by high impact. Dazed and shaken, the driver stood nearby with both hands on his head.

"Sayegusa boy," Conchita whispered. "He da one drive dat red Studebaker all da time." Her voice sounded peremptory.

Kaz nodded. "Look like he okay, eh? Lucky buggah!"

"Goin get hell for sure. It not his car," said Conchita blowing a stray lock of hair from her face.

"Not his car?" Kaz echoed.

"Belong his papa."

"How you know?"

"How he get enough money working at Bernie Abe's garage?"

"No pay money?"

"Oh, Bernie pay money all right, but Sayegusa boy he jess graduate from high school."

"Young squirt, eh?"

"Yeah, fool around type. I see him wid Chu girl at Paradise bar like he own da place."

"You mean da Chu's youngest girl, da one wid hair like one bush?"

"Dat's da one. Her older sister go wid one army sergeant, nice guy. But da number two sister, she no good."

"Oh, yeah?" Kaz's puzzled look invited further elaboration.

"Get in trouble wid da police."

"What she do?"

"One time she bust up wid her boyfriend. She scratched up his car wid one key. Den she say she not da one."

"Den what?"

"Too bad, da Aki boy, Tony, him see her do it. Den she no can lie."

Kaz erupted into laughter, wiping her eyes with kleenex.

By now a handful of neighbors had run from their homes to investigate the matter. They stood in a semi-circle around the damaged heap.

"I donno how come." The Sayegusa boy offered a limp explanation to Joe Watson, retired cop. It was Joe who had called the police.

The young Sayegusa boy called Lefty was shaking his head. His eyes looked bloodshot. The women overheard Watson suggesting his brother's B & E Tow Service when an on-duty cop arrived. First he acknowledged Watson with "What's up?", then proceeded to fill out an accident report form as he questioned Lefty. Representing the boy — the only one at home at the time — grandma Sayegusa stood quietly in the shadow of a kukui nut tree. Her face was screwed up tight. She looked like a midget surrounded by giants.

Willy Fong who had been cruising by the neighborhood in his taxi-cab, joined the now animated and vociferous group. Each expressed an opinion of how the accident happened in the first place.

"He no look where he goin," one observer pontificated.

"Dey shudda cut down dese trees long ago," another suggested. "What dey good for anyhow?"

"Sometime hard to see. . ." a third said.

"Dis kind car no last long, dats for sure."

"Same teeng happened to my uncle two years ago, same teeng."

"Dats why I take da bus. I no like drive."

When they sidled up to Lefty, all he kept repeating was "Yeah, yeah." They smelled liquor on his breath, so everyone knew why the cop took Lefty in for futher questioning. Only grandma Sayegusa looked upset at his leaving. Still, she didn't utter a word. Lefty's breezy glance in her direction offered no comfort. No one spoke to her as they all knew she did not speak English.

Meanwhile Conchita and Kaz were standing by, taking in all of the rumble. Conchita nudged Kaz. "See dat fellah over dere wid da polka dot shirt?"

"Da green one?"

"Yeah."

"Ain't he friend of Emma Sing?"

"I donno but he one buggah to look out for I tell you."

"What he do?"

"Dat fellah over dere he sell me one stinking old fish, dat's what! He work down at Alawai Market. Last week I buy fish dere for my aunty Josephine's golden wedding anniversary. I make one good dinner wid her favorite chicken and pork, coconut pudding — all kind stuff — every teeng good but da fish. I tot I saw da red eyes but he say 'Oh, no, dese guaranteed fresh. Came in today. You lucky.'"

"He lie, eh?" said Kaz.

"I no buy fish from him again, the buggah. Burn me up."

"Some people have da nerve."

"I feel like giving one piece of my mind right now!" Conchita said.

"Forget it. Ain't goin do anyteeng."

By now only a handful of onlookers were left as one by one they returned to their respective homes. Slowly Conchita and Kaz too ambled back to their laundry.

After hanging up six pairs of boxer shorts, Kaz stopped to rest. She looked at the trees in Conchita's yard. Beside a mountain apple stood lichee and macadamia nut trees. The sour sap tree was heavy with fruit. Spiney and green, the globes looked like sea urchins. "Plenty sour sap, eh?" remarked Kaz.

"Dis year too much," said Conshita. "You want some? Pete Chan own da house. He planted da tree."

"You get enough?"

"Sure, we get too much. I pick some for you. Soft now, good for eat."

Conchita ran into her house to get a brown bag, then she knocked down about a dozen sour saps, filling her apron with their weight. She handed the filled sack to Kaz over the fence.

"Tanks. My husband Masa sure goin like dese," said Kaza.

"Help yourself anytime," said Conchita. "How you girl Hazel doin in dat business school?"

"She doin good. And you folks, how your muddah doin?"

Conchita flapped her hands like a bird about to take off. "Da doctor say she gotta watch what she eat — cut out chile pepper. Dat what she hate da most of all — no moh hot stuff. Stomach no can take."

Kaz sympathized, "Gee, too bad."

"Yeah, and she hurt her back da udder day too. Right now she resting. Gotta take it easy. Say, you know Mildred Lum?"

"No. I know Dolores Lum."

"Not da same. I was goin tell you she goin marry Jake Sanchez but you don't know her so nevah mind. . . . You know Mabel Kanashiro?"

"No. Wait, she sister to Dora Kanashiro, da one run beauty parlor up Liliha Street?"

"Not dat one. Mabel she in hospital now but you don't know her so nevah mind."

"And you boy Harry, still working for da army?" Kaz asked.

"Still dere. Harry and Emma now got five kids you know. Last one born last month. Three girls and two boys."

"Five kids," said Kaz, "Whew!"

"Dat what Harry says. He come over to do work sometimes, says he no can hear himself at home. Emma say 'Shut up' to da kids but dey no shut up."

Kaz laughed. She ran her hand over the sour saps she clutched. "Tanks again for dese," she said. Picking up a clothesbasket left in the yard, she made her way past a small grove of banana trees and climbed the back stairs leading to her kitchen.

She spent her afternoon making poha jam, ten golden glassfuls topped with paraffin. Carefully wiping them clean of syrup with a rice sack dish towel, she arranged them above the kitchen sink where she could admire their coughdrop color. Just as she was about to sit down and relax, her husband Masa entered through the back door.

"You home," said Kaz.

"Yeah, I'm home. Some guy said dere was an accident around here."

Kaz picked up a hairpin from the floor by her feet and slipped it into her hair casually. "Da Sayegusa boy. He bang up da car. Coconut tree in back his house by da Palumbo garage."

"He hurt?"

"Nah. He lucky."

"Police come?"

"Yeah, one come. I teenk Sayegusa boy drunk. Police took him back to da Kololo Street station."

"Figures."

"Yeah?"

"I know he one good for nuttin."

"Smart aleck, eh?"

"I know when he cut his hair in dat duck tail, long in back, he asking for trouble."

Kaz wrapped an apron around her then began cooking supper's pot of rice.

SPECTER

In a city, the odd man, ignored by most, can hide. But plant this same man in a small town and he will be a notable. In Lunalilo, such a man was Malcolm Stillwaite. My assignment was to interview him at his home. I had in hand a spidery map George Yuen, editor at the *Lunalilo Chronicle*, had drawn for me. I was to discover that without it, it might have been difficult to locate Stillwaite.

Aggressive in touting the town's few cultural events, he was first on society editor Henrietta Clabbard's list. Her idea was to run a six-week series profiling carefully selected champions of the summer bandshell concerts, laying the groundwork for a donation drive to follow.

Thus, on a premonitory, muggy, overcast day of fine drizzle, I began the ten-mile drive outside the city in an effort to reach this man, this eccentric as George described him. George's directions were easy enough to decipher while driving on well-marked paved roads, but at the end of Kalolo Drive, I faced with some trepidation a deeply rutted road marked simply M.S.Ln., seeming to disappear into a rugged thicket.

From this vantage point, I got out of the car to survey the prospect, and to assure myself that taking M.S.Ln. would get me somewhere. The tangle of towering weeds and trees festooned with wild philodendron vines, all dripping beads like a rosary, added to that day's miasmic atmosphere. I had not passed a house on Kalolo for several miles. Ahead, in the direction of the weathered, hand-painted sign, a hill, thickly treed, rose like a pinnacle. I imagined it marked "scenic lookout," facing as it did a steep descent to the sea. At the summit spreading curved wings like a sea tern, a house perched in solitary defiance of the surrounding green jungle. The labor, it struck me, must have been enormous, transporting every piece of lumber to that height. Still, the result was impressive and now, closer to my destination, I looked forward to the interview with renewed curiosity — once I had overcome the hurdle of the bumpy, gutted lane in my second-hand Ford. It was not going to be easy.

Patience was the operative I told myself as the car crept along a winding road past stately eucalyptus stands. At one point, I got out to remove a fallen branch from the roadway. This man must covet privacy in the extreme, I thought to myself, as I continued under a darkened overhang, like a shadowy canopy of rain forest. At one turn, I saw a gray, stone shrine with fresh flowers placed before it. It was my first sighting of human activity in some time and as such, though curious, was reassuring. More turns and more trees followed. Finally, small pebbles paved the winding road, indicating at last that the house must be near.

After the effort expended reaching the top, what greeted me appeared like Shangri-la. I parked, got out and made my way to an old, Kyoto-style structure, heavy with dark wood beams and spare lines. At what I surmised to be the main entrance, a suspended wind chime fashioned from bamboo tinkled in the breezy sussuration. In the distance, ocean sounds met this rise in the landscape, heaves and sighs of tremendous force.

Stillwaite obviously had expected me, for he appeared promptly with greetings, sliding open a *shoji* screen door, smiling as he pointed out the soft slippers for which I exchanged my shoes. Spartan in its simplicity, everything about the house maintained tradition. This bygone ambience felt strange, especially after the hectic newspaper office scarcely an hour ago. The dark interior had a calming influence, like floating on a sea with rain pelting one's face softly.

Clad in a dark brown *yukata*, Stillwaite himself, except for his white skin and Nordic features, embodied the oriental man lounging at home in a cotton kimono. My initial reaction was scepticism. This man's an actor, a very cunning actor whose carefully contrived manner convinces you that he is indeed Japanese! His eyes are slanted! Delicate in build, he moved his arms and legs as a man doing Chinese calisthenics. His use of gestures seemed excessive when he bowed from the waist after our introduction. I could see the bald top of his wispy, graying head, white folds of skin at the nape. His voice, cello like, meted out sentences as if in cadence. As he spoke he had a disarming habit of staring out the window, narrowing his eyes. When, however, he looked at you, his gray blue eyes were direct.

"You are here to paint my portrait in words." His speech was stilted. "That too can be fine art."

"Yes." I forced a smile. Something about the man was phony.

"Shall we go into a room with a view?" he asked, directing me past another *shoji* screen separating the foyer from a large room with windows framing a distant blue sea. He rushed to open the window and inhaled the incoming air in an exaggerated fashion. The view was an extraordinary treetop expanse in three directions with cliffs to left and a swift drop to an angry ocean. The room's only concession to modernity was a piano, while cushions and low tables indicated activity at floor level. We were seated close to the window. I could hear Stillwaite breathe.

Then came a rustle, the swish of someone wearing a silken kimono and soft padded thumps of one wearing *tabis* on a straw mat floor. A young girl, tray in hand, entered.

"Ah, here is Kiso with tea," he said.

She was a dainty teen-ager, dressed in a too elegant kimono for this occasion. The last time I'd seen such a sumptuous print of purple wisteria was in a museum exhibit. Her *obi*, burnished gold with a dull, inlaid pattern of leaves, set off by a thin, red-tasseled braid, bound her chest snugly. Where had this girl come from, I asked myself. Certainly she is an anomaly in Hawaii, dressed up like a geisha. I studied her obvious stiff, black wig, studded with ornaments like kaleidoscopic pieces, her rice-powdered complexion, even the carmine eye shadow. As she poured tea, the girl comported herself with stylized grace. Her lips, closed as Mona Lisa's, proferred the only hint of an otherwise inscrutable face. I wondered if she felt comfortable in her confined clothing.

After filling our cups, she glanced discreetly at Stillwaite, who dismissed her with a slight nod. Her exit was as noiseless as her entrance.

Turning to Stillwaite, I asked, "Your Kiso, is she a local girl?"

He laughed sardonically. "You wouldn't guess it, would you?" I detected a slight grimace whisk over his otherwise passive face. "But in answer to your question, Yes, she is a local, a farmer's girl in fact. Her parents raise sweet potatoes and peanuts on the *mauka*, mountain side of the island. Both parents are pretty elderly and she was an only issue for them; they doted on Kiso. She tells me they sheltered her from the wild ways of today's young."

"She is lovely." I remarked, sipping the tea.

"Indeed. She is the adorable Japanese woman, composed and un-complaining, courteous, quiet and pliable as putty."

"It was fortunate that you found such a girl — ."

"Not entirely the found object — I had some molding to do — a few amenities here and there. I suggested her appearance. Fortunately, on visits to Japan, I had collected the wardrobe, make-up and so on."

"You must have planned it then?"

"Exactly! Smitten with the country, I felt this was the only way to exist."

"I am impressed. But you are so isolated."

"Not really. I have my gods and other companions."

Not understanding this arcane remark at the time, I merely jotted it down in my ruled notebook. "And Kiso, does she live here too?"

"Yes, this is Kiso's home. But don't worry, she has Mondays off. She visits her parents faithfully."

"I see."

"Well then, let's get down to business," said Stillwaite, impatient for an agenda to our rambling colloquy. "You came, after all, to ask my opinions on the proposed summer concert series."

"Yes, why do you feel Lunalilo needs this music?"

He exploded in a lengthy explanation, voicing his enthusiasm, in truth hunger for such a project, stating his boyhood ambition to be a symphony conductor no less.

"Why did you not become one?" I asked, perhaps impertinently.

"My mother," he said, his tone shaded with petulance. "She wanted me to be a doctor. . . ."

"And you rebelled?"

"No, I actually enrolled in medical school — Harvard to be exact — lasted for two years. My Dad, he was a doctor. I wanted him to be proud of me."

"And then . . . ."

"What's to say — I had a complete nervous breakdown at the time. I went to Japan to cure myself." A break in his speech divulged nervousness.

"And it was there that you decided on a change of lifestyle?"

"I would not state it quite that way. It was there that my *real* life began. . . ."

"Are there other members of your family here in Hawaii?"

"No. All are dead. But I have ashes of my parents on this property."

"Really?"

"Would you like to see the shrine?"

A shrine, perhaps the one I had passed getting here? "Of course," I answered thinking a walk would allow me to sift over the several importunate remarks thrown my way, answers to which still rankled. Still, good manners kept me from asking. In contrast to Kiso, I must not appear too nosey.

Sliding open yet another screened partition on the west side of the house, Stillwaite led me past an assiduously manicured tea garden, complete with *torii* and red carp pond, fed by bamboo-piped water. "Kagemasu, my gardener, does an excellent job with the garden, wouldn't you say?" he asked.

"Wonderful," I said, noting the appropriate smooth boulders of a cunning footpath, bushes trimmed precisely to complement a stone lantern, and flowering azaleas lending brilliance but not dominance beside a miniature waterfall.

To the left of the garden, a path through bamboo groves led us to a circular clearing where a penitent Stillwaite bowed and clasped his hands in prayer before a shrine, a larger structure than what I'd seen along the access way. Central to the altar was a Buddha figure with gardenia petals strewn round it, flanked by thin, green incense sticks. Contained in an elegant, porcelain bowl to the left was a wood strip inscribed LH-YK.

It was difficult to believe that we were only ten miles from town. I felt transported beyond time and space amid the perplexity of this place, surrounded by looming trees, cloud cover and the humidity of impending rain. At that moment I thought I heard a faraway mysterious chorus.

"Do you hear those voices?" I asked incredulously.

"Yes," he said with scarcely a moment's hesitation. "The dead remain in the world, you know. They are all gods and their happiness depends on us the living." His voice was earnest.

For a second I imagined him in a saffron robe. "Look!" he interjected excitedly, pointing out a butterfly with incandescent wings alighting as if by design on an incense stick.

"How beautiful," I remarked, then added, "Yet how sad to think that its life is so short."

"Ah — ," Stillwaite's voice grew doughty, "But there's the rub, the beauty of life *is* its uncertainty." He paused before continuing, "Have you ever heard of a man named Lefcadio Hearn?"

"Yes, vaguely," I said, "Didn't he write a book called *Gleanings in Buddha Fields?*"

"The woman is knowledgeable!" he asserted as though I were a third person participant. "You must study Hearn, also known as Yakumo Koizumi. Hearn said 'Perishability is the genius of the Japanese civilization!'"

Recalling the clever, cheap, mutable toys made in Japan such as miniature umbrellas and wind propellers, I agreed though fearing that Stillwaite would consider my examples silly.

Standing in that spot, surrounded by eidolons of Stillwaite's past, listening to him speak of life being controlled by the dead, I could understand a little of why he had chosen to live in this manner, *as though he himself were an avatar of Lefcadio.*

We returned to the main building where Kiso had prepared a luncheon of clear soup, marinated octopus, shredded spinach, pickles and rice — light but adequate fare beautifully presented in cunning, small dishes of distinct design and color. I watched Stillwaite seated lotus-fashion on the straw mat beside the low dining table, his fingers deftly manipulating chop sticks of tiny morsels, transferring them to his mouth as a jeweler sets gems. Seeing Kiso again, questions remained as she silently performed her tasks, not for a moment betraying any emotion, in essence like the studied flower arrangement in Stillwaite's alcove.

After the meal, I wound up the interview with questions about his taste in music — which turned out to be heavily Baroque. Rising, he offered to play for me the piece sitting open on his piano. It was a Scarlatti etude which he rendered with flawless technique. Shaking hands, I thanked him for his generously given time, told him how much I valued the visit, and took my leave.

❄ ❄ ❄

Deciphering notes taken at the time of that unforgettable if puzzling interview, that brush with the supernatural, that contrived, bizarre ambiance, reinforced George's warning about the man being eccentric. It bothered me that I couldn't shake off the mystery. Either his dedication was fatuous or else we, the remainder of Lunalilo, were out of step with our drummer. Tenuously I sketched his profile, emphasizing his devotion to music which was, after all, the point and purpose of the interview.

The next day at work, George asked, "How did it go?"

"The interview with Stillwaite, you mean?" I replied, pleased at the opening to discuss the matter. "Well," I paused. "He is, as you said, eccentric all right. Do you know he has a maid who dresses up like a geisha? I mean the old-time courtesan!"

"Really?" George said, "That should make interesting copy."

"He has strange ideas about the ideal woman, no feminist, I tell you."

George laughed; the pencil behind his ear shook. I could see that the whole thing was a good joke for him.

"Okay. Okay, so I'll write it up making him appear an angel with good intentions so that people will donate lots of money to a good community cause."

"That's your job — go to it," George said, returning to his typewriter.

It was a Monday morning. As usual, I planned to pick up a hurried lunch at the popular Cadabona Good Eats Cafe across the street.

Sidling into my usual far end booth of the restaurant, I immediately scanned the menu which I knew by heart yet read again. "I'll take the soup and salad, number three," I told Sally the waitress.

Waiting for my order I took out a magazine and chanced to glance across the room. Three customers burst in laughing, a young girl and two young men escorts. They headed straight for the counter. To my astonishment, I saw that the girl was Kiso! Were my eyes deceiving me? I looked again. Gone was the wig! No pasty make-up; her hair, loose! Stillwaite's oriental manikin had become Miss Teeny Bopper!

The three carried on a banter of horseplay. From the corner of my eye I watched as she took puffs of a cigarette. She curved her arms round the smaller young man's shoulder, bending over to his side as she talked, surprisingly garrulous for a girl who had not uttered a single word during my visit with Stillwaite. But then, Kiso in this surrounding was totally unexpected, so convinced had I been of the role she played for Stillwaite.

"Hey, you guys, cut it out," she said. "We no fight you know."

"You goin' swim?"

"I said I would."

"Okay, den, eat up. We gotta go befo too late, eh?"

"No push me too hard, eh. I eat, I eat."

"So what else is new in Lunalilo?"

"You talk like you live out of town."

"I may as well — you guys don't know how weird my job is — ."

"Oh yeah?"

"Yeah."

"Like how?"

"You wouldn't believe it."

"Try us."

"Nah, it's too weird."

"Why you work then?"

"Pay's good."

"That's all folks."

"Good hamburger," said Kiso as she devoured her lunch, taking another sip of coca-cola.

THE HOLDUP

No sooner had Emily Yabuki, night shift cook at Kau Kau Korner, shuffled to work, netted her gray hair, and donned a canvas apron then Phil Villapando, flipping hamburgers on the grill, called out "Dan wants talk to you." From his importunate tone of voice, Emily guessed why Dan Yap, manager of Kau Kau, had made that request. The holdup, last night's holdup, she concluded.

Taking her sweet old time as usual, Emily finished wiping her forehead with kleenex, and peered into the kitchen mirror as if astonished to see herself there. "Oh yeah?" she said, "Bet he wants to know what happened, eh?" Her speech, languid as her general disposition, seldom rose above tepid.

"Too bad I was sick last night." Phil wiped hands on his apron as he spoke. "Missed one big show I heard."

"One really big show — " she repeated, rolling her eyes petulantly from ceiling to linoleum floor. "Goin make me famous — ."

"Not every night we get robbed!" Phil declared, enclosing browned patties into buns, adding slices of sweet pickles, placing a Hilo Krunch potato chip pack on each plate.

"You can say that again. We not Bank of Hawaii, you know."

"Stupid kid, eh, think he goin get rich — ." Phil switched from his usual banter to a sardonic vein. "I heard when Winnie handed over ninety-three bucks, the kid said, 'Is that all you got?' 'Sure,' she said, 'This Monday night — Monday's slow.' Funny, eh?" Phil shook his head, bending over as he laughed.

"Funny to you but not funny to Dan, I bet," Emily said. A crook of her index finger beckoned him. "Listen, between you and me, I think the guy knew one of the waitresses. These young squirts, you know."

"Yeah," he said, enthralled by her confidence in him.

"Ever notice how many young kids hang around this place?"

"Yeah," said Phil, amenable as a puppy.

"All up to no good." With a sneer, she trashed the bunch.

"Yeah," said Phil.

"Ever since Dan, things goin to pot — moh bettah in old days, I tell you." Emily splayed open the wood shutter door dividing kitchen from dining room as she sidled past plastic-made-to-look-like-wood tables, each topped with a vase of plastic flowers smack in the center.

Of the three waitresses on night shift, only Hazel Choy was busy taking orders from a lone, bald customer seated at her corner table. Against the fountain counter, Prudencia Corpuz and Winnie Kiso, young girls with hair blown over their foreheads as if caught in a gale, stood facing the front entrance. They waved to Emily. Acknowledging them with a smile and a bob of her head, she made her way toward Dan Yap next to a cash register. Nephew to Harry Goo, *real* owner of the place, Dan wore a uniform of white shirt, necktie and a no-nonsense demeanor. Phil had said the man never let his hair down, not even after a few drinks. Facing Dan, Emily was reminded of Phil's on target description.

"Hi, Emily," Dan said, refilling a toothpick container next to the register.

"Hi," Emily said, in her usual dead-pan voice. "You want see me?"

"Yah." Dan placed a stenographer's tablet before him on the counter. From his breast pocket he took out a pencil. "Did you hear anything last night when it happened?"

Emily's eyes were set on the kitchen door as though she longed to hurry back. "Not much."

"Tell me what — " Dan urged, rubbing the pencil's eraser with his thumb.

Her recounting began slowly, like a hand-cranked phonograph record. "Was quiet, eh. Monday's slow. So — so once in while I peek out to see who's eating. I saw one *haole* man, kinda old, not too old, sitting by himself over there." She pointed to the table window. "Had a tattoo on his arm."

"Then what?" Excitement enlarged Dan's eyes.

"Winifred was checking out the last customer, one Japanese man I think, the lame-on-one-foot — comes in for waffles all time — yeah, he's the one, I think."

"Then what?"

During pauses Dan twisted his large onyx university ring. Emily hated the brown monstrosity. She considered him a show-off. "Winnie was still at the cash register. Next thing we knew, this guy — not too tall, only a little bit taller than me — busted in with lady's stocking on his head. 'Stick em up,' he said to Winnie. I almost die laughing when I heard that — jess like ole time James Cagney movies, eh?"

Dan did not appreciate her side-tracking. This was not funny stuff. He nodded his head as if to humor a child. He noted Emily's wrinkles as she furrowed her brow. Should've gotten rid of her long ago he thought.

"Can't say if he had *real* gun for sure, but he pointed somethin like one black stick at Winnie. Then he asked for money. Everybody could hear her open the cash drawer and take out all the bills inside. Nobody moved except the guy. He put the money in his pants pocket, then ran outside."

"Wish I had been here," Dan said.

"Would have been different — " Emily said as her voice trailed off. How different, she didn't say.

"My one night off and this thing happens!" Dan drummed his impatience with pencil, stabbing the pad's margin.

"One more thing," Emily said, "the *haole* left right after. . . ."

"Yeah, but we can't be sure if he had anything to do with it."

Dan should have gone to law school, Emily thought. She knew Harry Goo once offered to pay for his nephew's education. He got a head on him. "That's all, eh, Dan?" she asked with one foot already heading back to the kitchen.

"That's all. Thanks." Satisfied or not, Dan's voice betrayed nothing.

All during the discussion, Hazel Choy had strained to hear them above the kitchen clatter. She stepped forward, confronting Dan. "She's right about the *haole* customer."

Dan continued writing while she spoke.

"He acted kinda queer — like he wanted to get out fast." Hazel enjoyed Dan's spotlight on her. He'd given her the glad eye on more than one occasion.

"You told this to the policeman? What's his name?"

"Mel Gomez."

"Yeah, Mel Gomez," Dan added. "Well Winnie did the right thing." He raised his voice to catch Winnie's attention. She was busy taking an order but her ear was cocked to Dan's talk. "She gave him the ninety-three bucks. She called the police. She did everything perfect."

Hazel faced him with an ineffable expression on her face. He isn't easy to talk to she thought. Everybody knows he fools around Winnie, everybody excepting his wife Iris but that's nothing new in town.

❊ ❊ ❊

Back in the hot kitchen, Emily began chopping onions.

From the deep, stainless steel sinks, Phil shook out a colander of freshly washed lettuce. He walked past a thick butcher-block table to where Emily worked. "What Dan say?" Phil popped the question in a hushed voice, cupping a hand over his mouth.

"Same thing." She shrugged her shoulders. "Nothing we can do about it. Was only ninety-three bucks you know. No big deal."

Phil never knew whether Emily's reluctance to talk was real or feigned. Deep down, he felt she wanted very much to talk. Still, she never really opened up to him. He asked, "Were you scared?" His curiosity gave him a little boy expression.

"Sure thing," she said emphatically.

"Yeah, I would be scared too — never can tell, eh?"

Out of the blue, Emily asked "Buster at work?"

"Yep," said Phil at a loss to understand Emily's concern for the lad.

After covering the sliced onions with waxed paper, she rinsed knife and cutting board immediately then took a kleenex from her apron pocket to blow her nose. Next, she sliced tomatoes. Phil shredded cabbage cole slaw. Momentarily the two cooks felt strangely coalesced as if in a kind of collusion against evil. Phil knew that Emily had worked at Kau Kau longer than anyone else. Moreover, she knew Harry Goo personally. Thanks to Harry, she was still working. When Dan took over, first off he hired young blood. There was always tension between Dan and Emily. Still, Phil felt more secure about his job, concluding that if she had worked here twenty years, he could last as long, even if she cooked better. Besides, he needed the money as sole supporter of his widowed mother. Spending little on himself — cigarettes being his only weakness — he prided himself on his bank savings. Once, he had even told Prudencia, the youngest waitress, exactly how much money he'd stashed away. His disclosure had puzzled the girl. Did he mean to impress her or what? Was this a proposal? She told Hazel about it and both girls, after much giggling, concluded that Phil was sometimes very strange.

Although he'd wanted to question Emily further on the matter, a fresh flow of diners kept both busy in the early morning hours that followed. The place was abuzz. Dan clanged the cash register while Prudencia, Hazel and Winnie hopped from table to table, from dining room to kitchen, nonstop. Finally, around three a.m., that hot, muggy hour, business trickled down to the more normal pace of one or two customers at a time. Leaning against the counter, the girls in their mustard aprons relaxed, indulging in one of their favorite pastimes, teasing Buster Beamer, a clean-up boy.

There was about Buster a look of farm-boy innocence, as though he belonged in overalls with his freckles and curly hair. This time the girls noticed his new shoes. They teased him about that. He told Hazel he had rubbed dirt on the toes so they wouldn't look so shiny. His work consisted largely of scraping clean and stacking each plate on the dumbwaiter.

"Hey Buster," Prudencia cooed in reedy tones. "Was that your brother with the stocking on his face last night?"

Winnie and Hazel tittered.

"I thought it was your uncle, eh?" was Buster's repartee. He knew the girls adored his ingenuousness. "Looked just like you," he added, returning to his scraping with more than usual aggressiveness.

Just then three customers broke up the girls' intermission. Winnie led the group to a round table in the center of the room. They were one man and two women wearing plumeria leis, obvious tourists. Their garlands were a dead giveaway, that and their untanned legs: shark bait, locals said.

"See what I told you, this is an eatery," remarked the pink and plump woman wearing a salmon colored dress styled like a tent.

"Honey," the bulbous-nosed man said, presumably her husband, speaking to Winnie. "What kind of name is Kau Kau (cow, cow)? My wife here is ignorant."

The two women laughed at his lambent humor.

"It's Hawaiian," Winnie answered politely. "Means to eat —."

"I get it," said the man, chuckling to himself. He scanned the menu. "Now Ladies, what'll you have? Honey, I'll try your Beachcomber burgers," he said to Winnie. "You girls made up your minds yet?" he asked the ladies. The two studied the menu as though cramming for an exam.

"I'll come back," Winnie snapped.

"Holy cow, how much time do you dames need?" His patience thinned as five minutes passed and still they couldn't decide. Finally from a dime-store sack he pulled out a toy pistol, aimed it at the two and shouted "Time's up!" Panic struck the place. Hazel and Prudencia yelled. Dan ran to seize the pistol from the startled man who in fright dropped the plastic toy to the floor. Red-faced, Dan picked it up and handed it back. "Sorry about it," he said. "We just had a holdup lately."

The man looked dumbfounded as everyone sighed relief and returned to life before the scare.

✳ ✳ ✳

Singly, after five a.m. at the end of their shift, the staff left. Dawn of the next day began as a faint, pinkish glow above the horizon.

Emily took the Alakai bus home to a neighborhood of modest homes squatting side by side. Her husband Shig, truck driver for Fujihara Trucking Services, was home. Since he worked late hours quite often, breakfast was their only meal together weekdays.

"Dan asked me about last night business," she remarked over a cup of coffee.

"Oh, yeah," Shig offered feebly, rubbing his eyes. He had stayed up too late watching the sumo special.

"Said they still don't know who the kid was."

Shig waved his hand as if to shoo away the possibility of ever finding him. "Dan still no suspect, eh?"

"No."

"You don't open your mouth, eh?"

"You think me stupid?" Emily gave him a look she'd give a dog with mange. "I told Dan about the man who was there before, the *haole* guy with the tattoo. Even Winnie said he looked funny, like he was guilty or something. When the kid called up, I told him to keep the money — he did his job okay." She fiddled with a flower pattern on the table's oilcloth, tracing its red outline with her index finger. "Other day Goo asked about Dan."

"Oh, yeah?"

"Dan no look good now." Emily, bobbing her head up and down, grinned. "Serves him right," she muttered.

Shig gulped down his coffee then stood up abruptly. "Well, gotta go now," he said. They exchanged nods, silent goodbyes, a part of their early morning ritual.

* * *

It took Buster Beamer a half hour on good days to ride his bicycle to and from work. He lived with his grandmother, Molly Beamer, in her run-down but comfortable duplex. The left side was where they lived, renting the other half to Bill Kamakahi and his latest girlfriend. Bill's job as merchant seaman kept him overseas more often than portside, yet every time Molly collected rent payments, a new *wahini* with or without the children greeted her.

Tuesday, after his so-called graveyard shift at Kau Kau, the morning after the holdup, Buster hiked home with a brown shopping bag containing two recently patched jeans. Laundered and neatly folded, they'd been mended by Emily Yabuki, the old cook lady who, upon seeing his holey pants as he bent over his cart, called him to the kitchen where she persuaded him to bring in any jeans needing repair. "No trouble," she said in her usual monotone. "I have plenty time to sew." And that offer began an odd but warm tie between the old lady and the youngster, as Dan Yap referred to Buster — a sometimes curious relationship which nonetheless was buttressed by mutual respect. Grandma Molly caught, from time to time, Buster recounting how Emily would save a hamburger for him in the kitchen. Molly always said, to whoever asked about her grandson, too bad his folks busted up the way they did, but his father was a bum, even if he was her son. About Buster's mom little if anything was said. So far as Buster was concerned, the Pacific Ocean separated him from his mom and her army sergeant plus their six kids in San Diego. Buster hardly thought about them any more.

Now he found Molly in the back yard, digging up sweet potatoes. Lately she had experienced trouble sleeping. "Granny," Buster shouted, "Guess what happened?"

"You didn't lose your shoes again?" Molly screwed up a face of disgust, a ploy he loved.

"No way. Guess again."

"I give up. You too smart for me," she said sweetly. If anybody, Buster could melt this tough old lady.

"There was this robber guy who talked to Winnie. Had a cover over his face. She gave him ninety-three dollars! How you like that?"

He was disappointed at her dispassionate reply. "Just like that, huh?" she said after running through Buster's sketchy account in her mind. She took a deep puff of her cigar, inhaling as though it sustained her life. "Nobody know this guy?"

There was little that could ruffle Grandma. She had seen it all, it seemed to him. "Nobody," Buster said. "He picked us cause we open twenty-four hours."

"Called the police?"

"Oh sure."

"Well then, let them figure out. It's their job." The old lady returned to her digging.

Buster noted that her wrinkled hands, caked with dirt, had veins looking like blue worms. He returned to his bike parked against the garage to get the sack he had left in the wire basket.

"What's in the bag?" Molly asked.

"Just some old jeans. Emily fixed them."

"Mama-*san*?"

"Yeah." She looked away, giving Buster no opportunity to read her face.

"You thanked her?"

"Yes ma'am."

"Nice of her." Molly puffed smoke toward the banana tree. "Say Buster," she dropped, as an after-thought, "You got new shoes for your birthday."

Caught by surprise, Buster grinned from ear to ear of his tan, freckled face. "What's to eat?" he asked.

"Corn flakes," came Molly's reply. "Bread's in the refrigerator," she tacked on, returning to her digging as Buster danced into the kitchen.

❊ ❊ ❊

On the other side of town, Phil Villapando parked his blue Bel Air in the driveway of a sagging, greenish-blue house enveloped by the umbrella of a huge monkey pod tree. His mother was outside the wash house, feeding Baby, their overweight black mutt.

Phil waited until he reached the back door before addressing her. "How goes it, Mom," he asked in a feckless voice. The old lady, aproned, with iron gray hair and leather-tanned skin, gave him a smile which consumed her face. "You home already — " she said as if to re-establish his presence.

"Yeah."

"Any more news about the robber?" Her voice cracked, she so seldom spoke to anyone all day excepting her son. Baby kept jumping playfully to her hips as she spoke. She re-directed the dog to his feed bowl.

"Nothing new," Phil said, his eye on Baby, "still I think the guy must have known Buster Beamer. I noticed he wore new shoes to work."

"So what?" asked his mother.

"So plenty — shoes not free, cost money — anyway, the kid is one smart ass I don't like. Wouldn't trust him any more than one snake, I tell you."

Phil either liked you or buried you, his mother thought to herself. That's how he always divided the whole world, even as a kid he did that. Still, he's one good son.

Phil stretched as he yawned. In his left hand he carried the morning's newspaper picked up outside the restaurant. "Maybe somethin in the paper if the cops aren't sitting on their *okoles*." He entered a dark kitchen through a screen door as his mother patted Baby.

✳ ✳ ✳

On his way home in a white Oldsmobile, Dan Yap stopped to talk to Henry Aki, best friend and classmate, owner of Speedy Dry Cleaners on Noni Way. Both men were of average height and weight, anxious and quick to smile. Their shoes were highly polished. They had consulted each other on every move of a business nature; by now it was a habit neither could explain. They just felt an obligation, after all these years, to let the other know. This morning was no exception.

"Hi, Hen," said Dan, "Early, eh?"

Henry looked at his wristwatch and rubbed his eyes as if reacting to what he saw. "On your way home?"

"Yeah."

"Hey, what's new on the robbery?"

"Nothing much."

"Goo not going make you cough up the loss, eh?"

"Naw. . . . One thing still bother me, though. Can't figure it out."

"What's that?"

"How did the guy know it was my night off? It's not like I take off every Monday. I think he musta got tip off from one of the girls. One

of them is new, you know, and she's got loads of friends — ."

"Come pick her up after work?"

"Well, she gets off five in the morning."

"Not your fault. One man stick up the place, happens every day. Plenty time. How's your wife Iris?"

"Good. She's back from the hospital."

"Tell her to get well, eh?"

"Will do that."

"How's Mew Lun, your aunty?"

"She's okay too. About the other thing, don't worry. Mel Gomez, police, take over now."

"Mel Gomez? For crying out loud, I know the guy!"

"Oh, yeah?"

"Sure, used to date Dolly Pung, work at Aloha Plumbing, secretary to the boss, Harry Yuen."

"Oh, yeah?"

"Mel likes fool around a lot, but inside, he's got heart."

Dan couldn't interpret Henry's curious statement.

"Been with the force for six years or so. But like everything else, this going take time."

Dan sank into his usual dark nihilism. "Can't expect anything."

"But say goodbye to the ninety-three bucks for sure." Henry's smile was a wicked leer.

"You ain't kidding."

"Well, lucky it wasn't more."

"Yeah, well, I gotta get going. Call me sometimes."

"Okay."

✳ ✳ ✳

The waitress Winnie Kiso, cute in an elfin way, twenty-four and already divorced, walked home to her apartment on Coral Reef Drive, only four blocks away. She had been fortunate to find a place within her meager salary and tips thanks to her boyfriend Andy Soon, whose uncle owned the seaside building. The two had met at Lucy Suh's wedding. Since that time a casual, non-verbal agreement held together by phone calls, joined them in a loose but steady "going together" despite their indeterminate work hours.

Of late, however, due to happenings at work, her faithfulness to Andy had shaken. Dan, that all-business guy, mentioned to Winnie in the narrow hallway separating the two restrooms, that he'd like to meet her Sunday, her night off. Hearing that, she about flipped. Imagine a pass from goody-goody Dan, of all people, especially since Iris was expecting again. Winnie felt chary of his solicitation. Her old standby motto that business and love don't mix suddenly applied. Unable to sit on her problem another minute, she decided to talk things over with Hazel Choy, who couldn't be in bed already, only twenty minutes past their quitting time so she dialed.

"Choy's," a luckluster male voice answered.

"Hi, is Hazel in?"

"Hazel? She working now — no. Wait a minute, here she comes this minute — hold on." He banged down the receiver.

Winnie buffed her fingernails while she waited.

"Hello." Hazel's voice sounded as though she were in a tunnel.

"Hey this is Winnie — Winifred from work."

"Winnie — oh that Winnie," said Hazel as though she rifled through a file of sixteen Winifreds.

"Listen, I know you're tired, just got off work, but I wanted to talk to you about what happened Monday night."

"Yeah, it's okay, I mean we can talk." Mention of Monday roused her interest.

"Good girl. Listen, Hazel, don't you think that stick-up guy sounded like Venny Ramones, Prudencia's ex-boyfriend?"

"You mean that part-time movie actor?"

"Yeah, he had a bit part way back that swelled his head. Ever since, he's been hanging around, too good for anything. I saw him once at Coco Beach bowling alley, acting like he was king pin, you know what I mean."

"Yeah." In order to get along with Winnie, it was best to agree about everything, Hazel thought, especially where the boss was concerned.

"Ven had that kind of voice, like he was swallowing his words."

Sometimes Winnie exaggerated too much, Hazel thought. "I never noticed."

"He was the kind of guy who would say something stupid like Stick em up."

"Gee, I donno. Lately, I've been so busy with hula lessons in the afternoon, I don't know if I'm coming or going." Hazel visualized their upcoming demonstration at Lehua Center, with Frank Kupihea's ukelele band.

"I know what you mean. I don't even have time for my shorthand class nowadays. But getting back to Ven, I swear it was him all right."

"What Prudencia say?" Hazel was fishing; she knew that she and Prudencia usually maintained a veiled alliance against Winnie. Because of Dan? Jealousy? She didn't know.

"She said she bet it was one of Buster Beamer's no-good friends. You know she's got it in for him ever since he spilled chile on top of her new accordion-pleat skirt."

Prudencia never did coordinate a blouse with that magenta skirt, Winnie realized. "What about the *haole* guy who was there?"

"I donno. He's some kind of wino in the dumps. Harmless though. Even though he drinks, ever notice how nice his manners are?"

"Now that you mention it, I guess."

"Sure, I think maybe he's a really nice guy with a nag for a wife stateside."

Hazel laughed. This is how *she* usually explained the burgeoning influx of ex-servicemen to the islands. "What Phil and Emily say?"

"Phil thinks it could be Buster's friend. Emily, I donno. She kinda suspects he's a boyfriend to Prudencia, you or me."

"No!"

"No lie. She thinks just cause we have friends drop by to chew the fat late at night, they must be crooks. She's got it in for us just cause we're young."

"She should talk — " Hazel grew petulant. "Ever seen her husband, Shig? He's one no-goodnick guy. He sure likes em young." She winked.

"No!" Winnie's expression grew puerile.

"I could tell you stories bout him make you hair curl! He works for Fujihara trucking, same as my brother."

Hazel yawned. "No kidding."

"Well, you must be tired so I let you go. See you tomorrow night at Kau Kau." Darn it all, Winnie said to herself as she hung up, all that yak-yak and she hadn't even brought up the problem of Dan Yap. Oh well, things are sure getting complicated and they haven't even nabbed the crook yet. Maybe it's better not to know. For once, Emily would agree.

TWILIGHT

ENDO-SAN'S LIFE is as tidy as his dresser drawer containing monogrammed linen handkerchiefs, their pressed capital "E" face upward next to socks (all black), to the left front. Behind them, undershirts and boxer shorts (all white) are folded into precise squares, compartmentalized as a tray of *hors d'oeuvres* — a place for everything and everything in its place, as the cliche goes.

Sauntering downtown in his impeccable bland suits, a distinctive tinge of gray around his temples and sideburns, he impresses people as a man who cradles a charmed life in the palm of his hand. "Dashing" is how women characterise him. His is the classic face of angular lines and the favored aquiline nose. Adorers can easily imagine him, in an earlier epoch as a swash-buckling samurai commanding respect and awe. Men friends conclude that his life has been dealt all aces. Owner of the popular Palm Grove Inn, a thriving business filled to the brim on any weekend, a view of the sea from every window, Tadashi Endo is one of the few wealthy men in town.

In his moderately imposing home, he has a devoted wife, who in turn dedicates herself to their two children, the elder a son and the other, a daughter, Franklin and Janet. Their home is sequestered from the road by mature banyan trees, with their elephantine aerial roots so thick they hide the house.

Highly regarded by clergy, sought after by promoters of community causes, he is indeed a soft touch for donations. He can afford the generosity; money is his medium. Life has dealt him a few low cards but, where money is concerned, picture cards predominate.

Despite the largesse, however, Endo-san is not always happy. A dark side to his life, known only to a handful of close frieds, festers as a personal ailment. The problem is that he is in love with a hostess at the Sakura Bar & Grill. Evenings after work, he is a regular, planted firmly on a designated stool with business peers. As the evening unfolds, his calm expression transmutes to one of sadness, increasing with each sip of *sake*. The problem is Sadako, source of pain as well as pleasure to him. Obligated to his wife Teruko, nonetheless their marriage, propped by twenty-six years' accumulation, the daily motions now a habit, belies happiness.

Ironically, he is chained to the most delicate female he has ever known. She is Sadako, an effervescent type of woman with a kewpie doll voice, high pitch and taunting, epitomizing the fawning female. She has made it a career to make men happy. Despite her western dress, she dispenses the exact skilled, schooled panacea of a geisha. To the out of sorts, she proffers flattery: "You look especially handsome this evening. It must be your blue suit, perfect for your complexion. Makes you look young. Isn't that right?" she asks the bartender.

The latter, named Goro, knows her presence at the Sakura is indispensible. Times when she does not works due to illness or personal reasons, he is plied with "Where's Sadako?". This fact is clear to Kishi-*san*, owner of the Sakura, who bends to her every whim to keep her there.

And while she parcels out her feminine wiles with egalitarian finesse that she belongs in a sense, to Endo-*san* is a tacit fact. Though she may entertain a customer or two each evening, ultimately her final hours are reserved for him. On a few occasions — such as the time they visited a circus, Endo considered their appearance in public risky. Lunalilo was too small. Meetings at the Sakura were safer for all concerned. Until the appointed time, he snarls with jealousy in his heart, vowing to whisk her away, the better to prove his exclusive, uxorious possession. Sadako knows this; still she cannot be certain. Meanwhile, they go through the conventions of lovers, night after night, swearing fidelity — albeit not exclusiveness — to each other forever. Night after night he departs, returning to Teruko.

As Endo ages, the dilemma festers. Ten years younger than he, Sadako's beauty blossoms; her clientele increases. At the bathroom mirror one morning, he notes evidence of age as he combs his thinning hair. And that deepening gutter between his eyes, is it a sympton of his jealousy?

Strange that Teruko ages too; her complexion an ashen dryness, her walk grown spiritless too. But Sadako, her face dusted with rice powder, eyebrows penciled and lips painted a blood crimson, remains the eternal porcelain doll.

Of late, he has taken to dawdling over his second cup of coffee, watching his children prepare themselves for school while he ponders why this perfect family does not satisfy him. Why does Sadako fill a void?

"Did you sleep well?" asks Teruko, approaching him as a servant. She has the same diffident voice she possessed as a little girl. Her father used to say she sounded like a lost child. Vulnerability lies transparent on her face. This morning she wears a simple cotton kimono, its gray softly afloat with amaranth blossoms. He grunts an answer to her inquiry. Chirps of sparrows are heard through the window. He realizes that she handles ninety-five percent of their daily problems. It has been that way since the beginning. His opinion is required only in dire situations. Meeting his own children in the hallway, he feels a growing estrangement. They are tied to their mother. Am I too late already? Yet, however earnestly Tadashi vows that he will spend more time at home, in two weeks he has lost the resolve, only to slip into his old ways.

He watches Teruko washing the breakfast dishes, then bustling about the room, wash rag in hand. Ever since the children shared their lives, she does not take pains to groom herself as she once did. Compared to Sadako, she has not kept up with the latest fashion. Sadako always seems to know what they are wearing in Paris. She is that kind of person. Time and again he has suggested to Teruko that she shop for pretty dresses, only to be dismissed with "later on."

An incident involving his son still rankles. He had run into him about to leave home, baseball and bat in hand. His eye had caught sight of a new watch on the boy's wrist. "When did you get that?" he had asked.

"Yesterday was my birthday, didn't you know? Mom says this gift is from both of you."

"Oh-h-h," stuttered Endo.

Next day he confronted Teruko with "Why didn't you tell me it was his birthday?"

"I didn't think you were interested," she said. "You're always so busy."

"What kind of father are you talking about? I care about all three of you!"

"Well then — " said Teruko, lowering her head, "It was my mistake then. Forgive me."

❋ ❋ ❋

On a particular Monday, weary from work at the office, work which nonetheless he does not delegate to others — he wound his accustomed way down Lilikoi Street to the Sakura. At the far end of the counter, next to the wall, he occupied his "reserved seat," so faithful is his patronage.

"Good evenig, Endo-san," he is greeted by Goro the bartender. They have been friends now for over twenty years. Goro does not need to ask what he wishes to drink. Laying aside the dish towel with which he had been wiping glasses, Goro fetches a tiny bowl and a flask of warmed *saké*. Endo grunts approval as he sips, then notices that Sadako is nowhere to be seen. "Where's Sadako?" he asks.

"Sick," answers Goro. "She not feel well yesterday too, but you know Sadako, she stayed until closing time. Today she stay home for good. Better she get well."

"Nothing serious?" Endo's voice cracks with consternation.

"Don't know for sure. Said she felt hot. Many people not feel good nowadays. My wife too, headache."

"The boss around?" asks Endo.

"Sure thing, he's in the office in back."

Endo leaves his stool and heads for the back hallway where a bamboo curtain divides public from private rooms. To the left he enters a small office where Kishi, owner of the cafe, sits tallying figures on an abacus. He looks up and smiles recognition.

"I hate to bother you," says Endo.

"No, no bother," says Kishi-*san*. "What you want?" he points to a cane-seated chair, gesturing for him to sit down. Kishi's white shirt is rolled up at the sleeves, a green visor juts from his brow. Noisily puffing a cigarette held in discolored fingers, he clicks with efficiency.

"Sadako," says Endo, jumping to the point, "I hear she's sick, eh. So can you give me her home address? I go see her for myself. Maybe take some flowers." He smiles self-consciously, flashing a gold tooth.

Kishi, a businessman, veteran of ups and downs, nods his approval. He is worldly wise. His stingy smile reveals tobacco-stained teeth. From the desk's right hand drawer he pulls out a ledger marked Workers, scans a list mumbling all the while to himself "Sadako, Sadako Yonemura, 275 Mamo Street. Her apartment upstairs."

"No telephone?"

"No, no telephone. If you need call her, leave message with Mrs. Mukai downstairs, neh?"

"Thanks, I'll drop in to see if she needs anything."

"She like that," concludes Kishi. A smirk on his face signals total understanding.

✳ ✳ ✳

After purchasing a cluster of giant white Fuji mums which the florist arranges with maiden hair at the Murasaki Garden Shop, Endo drives to 275 Mamo. Parked in his Packard, he eyes a gray, two storey apartment building. Surprised by its dingy, run-down facade, he had expected something better of Sadako, ever scrupulous of her appearance. Surely she can afford a nicer neighborhood. He climbs scuffed wood stairs to the second floor and knocks on a door bearing her name. After a short interval he hears scurrying on the other side of the door, Sadako appears. She wears a dull, russet cotton kimono. Her face is rosy, as though she has just stepped out of a hot *ofuro.*

"Endo-*san!*" she exclaims, fastening her robe's sash, "Come, come inside." She gestures a welcome with both hands.

He hands her the flowers which she places on a table. Since this is his first visit to her apartment, he understands her excitement. "How did you know where I live?" Her voice actually squeaks; she appears flustered, disoriented by this surprise visit.

"Kishi-*san* told me."

"So — so — so." She titters as she speaks, nervously cupping laughter with her hand.

"Goro tells me you sick."

"Goro, neh," she repeats.

"Not the same without you, you know."

"Oh? No lie?" Her expression turns impish. Teasing again; one of her ploys.

"No lie," he repeats, studying the way her lips part like a bow. She jiggles ringlets dangling around her face. They sit on a tufted sofa. To the left he glimpses a small bedroom where books are strewn on a flowered *futon.*

"I make some tea?" asks Sadako.

"No — no need."

"Sure?"

"Sure," he repeats.

"One minute," she says, "I look awful. I go comb my hair. You shouldn't see me like this. Shame."

"No need," he insists, waving his hand for emphasis with no success as she scurries into her bedroom.

With Sadako out of sight, he has time to study the room's furnishings. What he sees on one wall rouses his attention. It is a collection of photos. He is taken aback to see so many of himself as well as both of them together, arm in arm at a circus they attended, side by side at the Sakura, feeding each other ice cream. She has even tacked up his graduation picture. The display roils guilt in him. Why does she need to reveal to the world that we are lovers? He shakes his head as if to deny this relationship. Until this moment he had not guessed the importance she places on him. Who else has seen these? Now he worries. To the left he sees a lone photo of a boy, a teenager he would guess in a kind of dark military uniform with buttons down the front. "Sadako," he calls out, "Who is this boy?"

"Oh him," she answers. Her tone of voice is strained as she swallows her words. "Yes, he is a boy."

"I can see that for myself. Who is he anyway?"

She stands beside the bedroom door. "He's my son," she confesses. Hand over heart, she clutches as if to stop the beating inside.

"What?" he stammers, "Tell me again."

"He's my boy!" She avoids his eyes. "I didn't think you would like to hear about him — anyway, I sent him back to Japan. Long time ago. My mother takes care of him on a country farm."

"Do you write to him?"

"Yes, I send him money too. He's happy over there."

"I see," mutters Endo.

"Anyway, you don't need to worry about him. He'll stay in Japan. That's the best all around. Best for everybody."

He is left speechless by her disclosure. She completes combing her hair then changes into a florid kimono, a purple one of wisteria blossoms.

✳ ✳ ✳

Hours later, Tadashi leaves her apartment, descending the wooden stairs. He sits inside his Packard, slumped back, trying to regain some sense of stability. He is tired. Across the street he eyes coconut trees, outlined by twilight. The sun, sunken over the horizon, leaves a faint glow the color of persimmon. Folklore says it is the time between cat and dog.

A wave of melancholy washes over him, recurrent as the seas, heaving back and forth, backward and forward. He thinks about Sadako, how little he knows her. And what of his own family? Who is he fooling? In his heart he feels a dull ache as inexorably dusk falls, blurring the palms from sight.

JESSICA KAWASUNA SAIKI

grew up in the Japanese-American community in Hawaii. Her critically acclaimed, first collection of short stories, *Once, A Lotus Garden* (New Rivers Press, 1987), is set in that community, just before and during the Second World War. The book was named by *Publisher's Weekly* as one of the nine best trade paperbacks of 1987.

Ms. Saiki, a longtime resident of Watertown, Wisconsin, has recently moved to Denver, Colorado. In addition to writing, Ms. Saiki is also an accomplished artist.